Jimmy's

Joseph Thomas Gatrell

Published by Joseph Thomas Gatrell, 2023.

For Mary Ann, Mary Ellen, Doreen, Sue, and Marci. We laughed. We cried. We took a few lumps, and we dished out a few. Somehow we survived. We're happy.

Jimmy's

Joseph Thomas Gatrell

Foreward and Acknowledgements

Life becomes simple when we condense those good things we keep. It reduces clutter, gives us room to maneuver, and provides accomplishment and fulfillment. Hence Jimmy's is a delicious stew of experiences and stories, some heard and others overheard. As the years passed, all of the aforementioned simmered together with no particular plate or place at the table. When will everything be ready? How will it be served?

Jimmy's was conceived many years ago when funny, repulsive characters became etched on the brain. A few things they said and did over the years were supplemented by embellishments and a few more characters. All were thrown into the crockpot and stirred together. Do you ever laugh when you cook?

As for acknowledgements, *ahem*, how could there be any? None of these characters are based upon real people. None of this ever happened. They are too far out of the mainstream. The scenarios are too improbable. Should you think you recognize someone or that you may have been in one of those situations, however . . .

Shame on you!

Joseph Thomas Gatrell

February 17, 2023

The Dream

The Dream always is the same. My Love and I are head over heels. Her beauty is of the magnitude that she charms the wildest beasts. This proved to be the problem. Upon learning of her beauty, the ruler of The Netherworld sent his henchman to snatch her. This he did while I was away. He took her to their kingdom below the earth. I had heard whispers that the Ruler of the Netherworld planned to steal My Love, but I did not believe them. Why should I? We were enraptured. Nothing could affect us, touch us.

When she disappeared without a trace, however, I understood the whispered warnings were true and that only someone with supernatural powers could have taken her.

What few above ground knew was that any mortal could venture to The Netherworld. Its ruler encouraged it so that he could outwit anyone who did so and steal their soul. Those few foolish to have done so had indeed lost their souls. Yet I had to take a chance. I could not live without My Love. So late one night, I went to a dark and an unsavory place. I opened a door. I walked down a stairway and through another door. There it was. The Netherworld. I entered.

As I expected, it was foreboding. There was only dim light, not friendly or flattering, but orange and gray, as though there were a distant fire during a depressing sunset. No one ever would desire to be in The Netherworld by choice, and no one with a soul would want to stay there. Despite the darkness, however, I noticed on the periphery that there was beauty. This both surprised and alarmed me, and it jolted me into the reality that mine was not the only Love The Ruler of the Netherworld had stolen. He had stolen loves and beauty from others. Thus I realized my love and I indeed were in eternal danger. That so much love and beauty was in The Netherworld meant attempts to reclaim them had failed. No sooner did I understand all of this that I began to hear wailing. It was those very souls. They were trying to warn me.

After the wailing had begun, I heard a growl. The wailing ceased. A voice asked, "Why have you come to my kingdom?" The voice was a growl. It sounded threatening.

"You know why I am here," I told him. "I wish to reclaim My Love and return her with me to the world above ground.

The Ruler of the Netherworld did not lie to me. Why should he? I was in his realm, and he had My Love in this vast darkness somewhere. For me to simply grab her and escape would be impossible.

The growling voice resumed. "Do you have anything to bargain with? Perhaps you would do me a favor. You could return to your world, steal something of great value from someone else while they sleep, and bring it to me."

The prospect was unacceptable. I could not victimize anyone. To expect me to take advantage of anyone whose plight I understood so well was absurd. The one thing I had come armed with, however, was knowledge of the Ruler of the Netherworld. According to legend, his love of games almost was equal to his greed and selfishness. I offered a proposition.

"How about a game of chance? If I win, My Love and I are free to return to our world, never to be bothered again by you."

"And if I win?" came the growl.

I conjured up my best brave smile and told him. "I do not plan to lose."

This time the growl was closer to a tiger's purr. "In that case, the bet shall be your soul. Do you accept?"

"Yes, I do accept as long as I am allowed to choose the game."

Before The Ruler could respond, there came a voice from behind a rock, or perhaps underneath it. It warned, "Do not trust him! It is a trick!"

I decided this must be the creature who, at the bidding of The Ruler of the Netherworld, the Henchman who had ascended to the world of light just long enough to steal My Love. It was an evil creature that sold their soul or bargained it away and now lived in the darkness far below the earth.

I ignored that voice and countered. "Surely I could not outsmart you, and I do not gamble. All I know is one simple game."

The Ruler sounded interested. "And what is that?"

"It is a game I have seen played on the streets. Is it simply called "shells"?

"Describe it."

"I will take three shells and a pebble from the ground. I will place a pebble under one of them. If you can select the shell that conceals the pebble, you win. If not, My Love and I will leave."

This time the voice was louder. "Do not be fooled by this! Let me take hold of him. We will keep both of them here!"

The Ruler of the Netherworld could have attempted this when I arrived. So I suspected his love of gambling was more than legend. It was fact. Gambling is a subset of greed. It allows creatures to use devious means to get what they want. Who could be more devious and greedy than The Ruler of the Netherworld?

The Ruler took the bait. "Choose three shells and a pebble from the ground. Then show them to me."

I did as he instructed.

"Now set them on the flat rock fifteen paces forward."

Again I did so.

The Ruler said, "Let us begin the game."

"It is a trick! Don't do it!"

I ignored the Henchman and began to shift the pebbles round and round, slowly at first. Faster. Then very fast. Intermittently I stopped and raised the shell with the pebble for The Ruler to see. Finally, after a great deal of movement, I announced, "Under which shell is the pebble?"

"Do not answer! I implore you!"

I took a deep breath. I waited.

"First I must see the pebble," The Ruler of the Netherworld growled. "I know you would not consider cheating me. That would be a violation of our bargain. It would cause you to forfeit your soul."

"I would not dare to try to fool you," I assured him, and I raised the center shell and showed him the pebble. "Satisfied?"

He growled ascent. "Proceed."

"Now I must be satisfied that you will honor our bargain. Bring out My Love. She must be next to me. We will win or lose together."

The Ruler of the Netherworld growled to the Henchman. "Do as he asks."

The Henchman oozed out from behind the rock, and it was more pathetic than I could have imagined. It was in the form of a man: tall, emaciated, and pale gray. It had long, wispy gray hair, and it was dressed in rags. Neither warmth nor positive energy emanated from this creature. Obviously it did not possess a soul. The Henchman disappeared into the darkness, but it quickly re-appeared with My Love. Just like that she was next to me, and I felt a surge of positive energy and confidence. I glared at the emaciated creature. With colorless eyes, it returned my glare before slinking back from whence he had come.

As I stared into the eerie light, I announced to The Ruler of the Netherworld, "I am ready. Are you?"

"Yes, I am ready to add your soul to my collection for all eternity." The words were followed by a sinister laugh.

While I was not a gambler, I was quick and very good at sleight of hand. Again I moved around the shells, briefly stopping to raise the one with the pebble for The Ruler to see. Finally all the swirling motion stopped. It would have been the moment of truth had there been any truth involved.

"Choose," I told him. The silence that followed seemed to last forever.

"It is under the shell on your right."

I knew it wasn't, and I quickly raised the shell to show him. We had won! I grabbed my love, and we quickly began to ascend back to the world above ground. As we did so, I heard the voice of the flunky.

"He cheated you! See!"

I knew what it had done. The Henchman had emerged from its rock, slinked to the shells, and raised the other two. It discovered there was no pebble - it was in my pocket - and alerted its master.

There came tremendous thunder and lightning from below. Winds swirled and howled beneath us. The Ruler bellowed, "Stop them!"

I knew the story of *Orpheus and Eurydice*. Ours was similar though not exactly the same. Nevertheless, I cautioned My Love, "Cling tightly to me and do not look back. I will glance back, but not directly at you until we are back in the Light World." I was taking no chances.

This helped us go faster, and every second of speed proved essential. Once I briefly glanced back, and I saw rolling dark clouds gaining on us. I knew if they caught up to us, their negative energy would take us prisoner and return us to The Netherworld for eternity.

Just when the clouds were about to envelop us, when they were so close I could feel the force their energy upon us, we burst through into the light above ground. When the clouds reached the surface, they dissipated. In the fresh air of The Light World, they had no power. The creature had stolen my love only because he had sneaked in and overpowered her when I was not present.

I hugged My Love. As I did so, I heard The Ruler of The Netherworld call to me, "I adore beauty and want her for my collection. Give her to me, and I will make you immortal."

"Love is eternal," I told him. "The type of immortality you offer is not."

From out of nowhere, his Henchman appeared. He hissed, "I will get her. You cannot be with her twenty-four-seven. I will take her again, and you never will get her back!"

I removed the pebble from my pocket, held it up, and announced, "Take this instead!" I threw the pebble at him, striking him in the center of the forehead. Though it was a mere pebble, the positive force of the pebble propelled the weakling backward into The Netherworld. My Love and I heard him wail a fading "Noooooo!" At last, the threat was completely gone. We were together and free.

Suddenly I heard loud, angry barking. I turned to view a new threat, this one earthly. Two dogs, one a great dane and the other a chihuahua, were charging toward us, barking and snarling. My Love and quickly I fled.

The chase was similar to our escape from The Netherworld. We moved quickly, but the dogs gained on us. Even the chihuahua, small as it was, ran at a speed more characteristic of a larger and more athletic dog. It went stride for stride with the great dane. They bared their teeth, of which the incisors were exaggeratedly large, so large that if they did catch us, they would rip us to shreds.

As My Love and I reached our home, they virtually were on our heels. We had escaped The Netherworld. Were we about to be caught by two angry dogs in the real world? I grabbed the knob of the front door and turned it. The door opened. The dogs hurled themselves at us.

That was where the Dream always ended, and I awoke, sweating and anxious.

Chapter 1
Dogs, B.O., and an Inkling

The following occurred quite a few years ago when things were different in the country and the world. Times and situations change, but people are the same. They always were, and they always will be.

As for those situations and the characters plugged into them by fate and bad decisions, the involvement of yours truly can be traced back to the appearances of The Great Dane and The Chihuahua. Not the title of a cartoon show or a fable, The Great Dane and Chihuahua were characters in another type of story, however, one that eventually became so improbable that were I not involved myself, I might not believe it.

As for those title characters, they were two aggressive young women with agendas, which was gutsy considering they were rookie teachers at stodgy male-dominated Bill O'Reilly High School in southwest suburban Chicago.

Perhaps because they were rookies and probably because they were in need of money, the women agreed to serve as cheerleading coaches. The Great Dane, a math teacher, was head coach. The Chihuahua, a physical education teacher and former gymnast, served as assistant. As a teacher and assistant basketball coach at B. O. High, I was able to catch some of their routines firsthand. Those two young women and their minions gave some improbable and thought-provoking performances.

They had received their nicknames for obvious reasons. The Great Dane was tall and lean but muscular. She had a thick mane of luxurious blond hair and was fair skinned. Reading her was an issue because when she spoke, which was rare, she did so in a husky voice that was emotionless and because her expressions seemed never to change. Staff members who'd been in a meeting with her would say, "I couldn't tell if she agreed or disagreed. She didn't say anything, and she seemed to be angry." Yet The Great Dane always stared very hard at the person speaking to her. This people found unnerving and intimidating and caused everyone to take her very seriously. Staff members spoke to her only when absolutely necessary.

The opposite was true for The Chihuahua, who enjoyed talking to anyone and everyone, and who the staff went out of its way to have a conversation. She was cute and flirtatious. What endeared her to every member of the staff, not only the men, were her frequent malapropisms, which did not discriminate. They truly were enjoyable for all.

The first malaprop was the most memorable. It came during a conversation in the staff room during which a teacher of humanities mentioned that her lesson was on the Greek tragedy which told the story of the newlyweds separated first by the death of the wife and again finally because, after winning her release with his irresistible music, the husband was hasty during their return to earth.

During high school, The Chihuahua read the story of *Orpheus and Eurydice*. That was not quite what she explained in the workroom that morning after listening to the humanities teacher. The Chihuahua looked up from the stack of papers she was grading, interjected how much she had enjoyed reading about "Orpheus and Uterus," and returned to what she was doing.

I was present that morning. The rest of us also looked up and at each other, and we held our gazes in stunned silence. Had we just heard correctly? Oblivious to what she said and our reactions, The Chihuahua stood up and left the room, after which he buzz began. It stopped when she burst back in and announced with a sheepish smile, "Of course I meant Eurydice!" At which time, everyone enjoyed a few laughs, including The Chihuahua.

Another time, at a post-game party during which receiving a compliment about her squad being precise in their performances, The

Chihuahua attributed it to a tip she had received. She explained it thusly: "After I learned that and incorporated it into our practices, the Red Sea partied."

The group she was in, of which yours truly was a member, was caught off guard. No one laughed, but we exchanged puzzled looks. The Red Sea did what? No one was sure if it was a Biblical reference or about the Red Sea Rivera. Before we were able to figure it out or ask her, The Chihuahua rambled on to something else.

On another occasion in the staff lounge, there was a lively discussion on political history. The Chihuahua walked in on it, paused to listen, and confidently interjected that "Bill Clinton was erected thanks to his persuasive personality." That drew a few laughs, including from The Chihuahua, who quickly realized her mistake, said, "Oopsie," giggled and apologized. The funny episode put the faculty on notice that you always listened to The Chihuahua because you never knew what would come out of her mouth. Had she known she was not taken seriously, she might have described it as "the icicles on the cake," which was how she had described the last in a series of bad luck events that had befallen one of her relatives.

In summary, unlike the intimidating Great Dane, The Chihuahua was at funny and easy to talk to if not understand. As time went on, she would prove to be intelligent and ultimately downright crafty.

Things meteoric start with a flourish. So it was with the Great Dane and the Chihuahua at B. O. High. Warned by their assigned mentors - both of whom were older males near retirement - that new teachers needed to lay down the law, each was incredibly demanding from the first day of school. This was before the Age of Educational Permissiveness, when all students became known as beautiful little children, and adult voices were not to be raised to them. The Great Dane and The Chihuahua, unrestrained by philosophical nonsense - or little else, as they eventually would prove - had an intimidating effect on their students, so much so that they quickly became villains to them. This gained them the immediate respect and admiration of the ultraconservative B. O. faculty, who believed that any teachers complained about by the enemy, i.e. the student body, had to be doing things right. During the first month of the school year, first The Great Dane and subsequently The Chihuahua were named "Bill O'Reilly Outstanding Teacher of the Week." For this, their names and photos were put on the marquee and video screens, and they were allowed to park their cars in the preferred parking space with the silhouette imprint of Bill O'Reilly near the entrance. This was a really big deal to the older staff members at B.O., who really believed parking in that space was part of a rite of passage. They said to the person who'd gained access, "You're in the parking space! You *are* B.O.!"

Perceptions and rites not withstanding, The Great Dane was no more than a dull math instructor who piled on homework, while her diminutive counterpart was a high-energy, exercise freak who refused to cut any slack to students in Health or P.E. classes. Each woman was more demanding in cheerleading than they were in the classroom. Practices were challenging. The Great Dane put her varsity squad through training that included martial arts, while The Chihuahua aerobicized her junior varsity group into top physical condition.

Top physical conditioning was a goal and a tactic. It was culling the heard. Candidates not up to the task quit or were run off. The strongest survived. A benefit was that cheerleading routines became more exciting to watch than episodes of "Survivor" because they were risky to perform. That season, the cheerleading won awards on the varsity and JV levels. A downside: going into the season, it also had more injuries than the football teams.

Nevertheless, The Great Dane, The Chihuahua, and their minions were well-prepared for opening night, a. k. a. the first home football game of the season. Spectators marveled at how athletic the cheerleaders looked – the word "svelt" was thrown around by some spectators - and how skillfully and precisely they performed their routines. After the game, the Great Dane and Chihuahua shook many hands and received great compliments. The game had been their coming out party, and it was a smashing success.

High school sports have traditions that go far beyond the athletic fields. The Great Dane and The Chihuahua participated in another when they were invited to a post-game celebration at the home of the B. O. High athletic director and his wife. The Great Dane and The Chihuahua arrived at the party over an hour late, however, and when they walked in, they argued loudly.

The Chihuahua insisted they were late because the Great Dane didn't know the way and got lost. The Great Dane was adamant it was the Chihuahua's fault because she'd disappeared somewhere after the game and kept her waiting. This was the first inkling anyone had that The Great Dane and The Chihuahua were not on the same page. The bickering went on throughout the season as the rookie co-workers alternately argued – often publicly and sometimes acidly – and patched up their differences just enough to co-exist.

The second inkling occurred after the last football game of the season. Afterward, the two women went barhopping with some of the football coaches and athletic boosters. The group became quite intoxicated ("roaring drunk" was a term I later heard in the faculty lounge) and ended up at the home of one of the coaches. According to the police report, things came to a painful halt at approximately 4 a.m. when The Great Dane took offense to a remark made by one of the boosters and decked him, knocking out his two front teeth. It took The Chihuahua - who reportedly had disappeared with two of the assistant football coaches, a booster, and his wife - only a few minutes to get her clothes back on and hustle her partner out of there before things got any worse.

The evening over but their exploits well-etched in B.O. High lore, The Great Dane and The Chihuahua were not long for the world of education, where news travels fast and rumors travel faster. Crossing the line may be grounds for dismissal. Obliterating the line guarantees it.

The Chihuahua was gone first, but not before she allegedly made it through some of the B.O. athletics coaching staffs and a few members of the faculty, reportedly both male and female. She was reportedly dismissed because she was discovered canoodling with a member of the PTA, a youth minister, and a school custodian in a closet during a rehearsal of, appropriately enough, the school talent show. The custodian had the best response during his disciplinary hearing. He was able to save his job when he explained that he had entered the closet for cleaning supplies and became locked inside. The Chihuahua was fired for cause. The youth minister was defrocked by his church. He wound up managing a fast food restaurant. The PTA was disbanded.

The Great Dane survived a tad bit longer, but she was terminated after it became painfully obvious she had a difficult time taking direction from those in leadership positions and needed training in anger management. After several run-ins with administrators, she was fired after slugging the head of the Math Department, a devout Mennonite who in thirty years on the job had never so much as raised his voice to anyone. There was speculation that she would have survived the incident had she claimed sexual harassment. As they wheeled the man out on a stretcher, however, he passed The Great Dane in the hallway and called out that he forgave her. In response, she karate kicked the stretcher, almost knocking it over, then gave him the finger. That was the nail in her coffin.

Physical education teachers are easily replaceable. Morality is in the eyes of the beholder. After a brief interview process, The Chihuahua's P.E. spot was filled by a woman, married for twenty-five years and a mother of four, who was the wife of an executive board member of the local Republican Party.

Math teachers can be very difficult hires, and cheerleading coaches can be almost impossible to get well into the school year. Bill O' Reilly, the high school, not the disgraced former news commentator, had to scramble. The process played out longer. Eventually Suzie Chen took arrived on the scene. Even for a student of history and humanity as educated as yours truly, it was like advancing from an entry-level course to a Master's class.

Chapter 2
Pardon My French

Il y a des moments ou tu realises que quelque chose ne va pas.

It was immediately after school on a Monday, and I had just entered the athletic office. Stylishly dressed in a business jacket, blouse, and skirt, a brunette whose coif perfectly framed her face was seated facing me in one of the lounge chairs. Her tanned legs were crossed in front of her as she held a pen and a clipboard on her lap. There was a look of amused distress on her face when she looked up at me and said rhetorically, "Do they always make new hires fill out so much paperwork?"

She paused, pointed the clipboard, and added with a wry smile, "It's a test right? If the new person doesn't quit by the time they have completed all of the forms, they are the right person for the job."

To this day, I don't know exactly where this came from, but I replied, "Have you dotted all of the i's and crossed all of the t's? Il ne faut rien laisser au hazard."

Just like that, we connected.

"Vouloir c'est pouvoir." Setting the clipboard and pen she added, "J'ai termine." She stuck out her right hand and said, "I'm the new girl. Suzi Chen. Math teacher and cheerleading coach." She did a really cute biting her bottom lip bemusement before adding, "I suppose my job title would be glutton for punishment."

"You're speaking French, and you're not the French teacher. "Mes compliments a vous." I accepted her hand and introduced myself.

"Three years of French in high school and a semester in Paris during college," she explained and added, "Are you the French teacher?"

"Also three years of French in high school. Straight A's, but I passed on the semester in Paris because I was playing basketball. Almost went into art history and took some courses. Eventually I drifted into my major. I'm history."

"An interesting way to phrase it." She asked, "Was missing Paris for basketball worth it?"

"We made the Tournament and reached the Elite Eight."

"Starter?"

"Sixth man. It's the story of my life: jack of all trades but master of none."

"Except you speak French and have knowledge of art and history." She glanced at the clock on the wall. "Sorry to cut this short. The new girl has to be upstairs for a meeting. Orientation and all that. I am sure I we will see each other around school. Maybe grab lunch or coffee sometime?"

"Sure," I responded. She turned, opened the door, and walked out of the office. The door closed behind her.

Qu'avais-je fait? That quickly I had met the woman I wanted to spend the rest of my life with but let her get away. I stood there a few moments, thought about that, and shook my head. Fortunately no one else was in the office to see or hear how foolish I appeared. Suzi Chen was here for a reason, and the reason was not me.

After the recent Great Dane and Chihuahua disaster, the B. O. hierarchy needed someone who was squeaky clean, not Squeaky Fromme. According to scuttlebutt, Suzie had been Magna Cum Laude at U. C. L. A., where she double-majored in mathematics and sports management and was captain of the cheerleading team. Upon graduation, she took a job in management with a West Coast baseball team, but found professional sports "pedestrian," as she grew tired of being talked down to and hit on by the "shallow types" who played and ran Major League Baseball. She needed to be in a real situation with people who had values and goals. Wanting to achieve and determined to give back, after the season Suzi was in search of another position when a headhunter contacted her about the teaching and coaching openings at B.O. It included to an incentive to earn a Type 75 and move into a leadership positon: i.e. the athletic director was set to retire in two years, and assistant principals jobs always opened up. Where could it be more real than working at a high school in the Midwest? The only official information the staff received, however, was the perfunctory introduction at the weekly faculty meeting.

Please give a warm B.O. welcome to Ms. Suzi Chen, who will be a member of our math and athletics departments. Suzi comes to us from the private sector, and we are certain she will be a great asset to the B.O. community.

This was followed by the traditional "B.O. High Five," which consisted not of actual palm slapping but polite applause and finger snapping, after which Suzi rose, thanked everyone, said she would do her best, smoothed her skirt, and sat down.

Suzi always kept it simple. My thinking was more complex. She was the math teacher. Yet I was the one who extrapolated. I'd decided Suzi Chen was the perfect woman for me. It went beyond the physical. She was a quick-witted intellectual who spoke French.

When Suzie and I were together in the faculty lounge or when we just happened to be walking in the same direction in a hallway, I tried to impress her with complex topics such as news from the corporate or business world, and current events. One day in the lounge as I was working on *The New York Times* Crossword Puzzle, Suzie appeared over my shoulder and said, "Now there's one of my love hate relationships. The Puzzle is frustrating. Yet I always come back to it."

She sat down next to me, and we worked on the Puzzle, and it was fun Most days, we shared our experiences during passing periods in the crowded hallway.

"What is Harpo Marx real name?" Suzi asked one day on approach.

I knew that one. "It's Adolph. Chico was Leonard, and Groucho was Julius," I said as I passed her.

"Show off!" she called, as everyone looked.

Another day, she asked, "Can you believe that clue for 12 Across?"

"Obscure to say the least."

"Did you know they were involved?"

"Didn't know and didn't want to know."

How is that for romantic banter, and how could she possibly fail to see my assets as well as my upside? I actually began to wonder if we could have a future together. I had a pretty good upside. Or so I thought.

Okay, I was a history teacher and assistant basketball coach, but I also was on track to be head of the social studies department and the head coach. Each person in that position was near retirement. I had graduate in the top ten percent of my class in high school and college. I was well read. *A Savage War Of Peace* by Alistair Horne and *The Powerbroker* as well as the books by Robert Caro, just to name a few. One of the books by Caro brought me a bit closer to Suzi, or so I was believed, when she saw me carrying one of them.

"I met Caro a few years ago in L.A. at a media event. At the time, he was working on the book that just came out," she told me.

"You met the great man? The research Caro does for his books his comprehensive. I'd have been in awe."

"I asked Caro about his research-," beamed Suzi. "He told me that his wife is instrumental. She is his life partner in every way: wife, co-writer, and researcher. I was impressed by their relationship."

I was impressed that Suzi was impressed. Was she dropping me a hint?

At that point, I needed one, but it wasn't about relationships. My life was about to take a very unexpected turn.

Chapter 3
Thirty Minutes to Vacate

While I had few bad habits, there was one that should have been a concern. I gambled. At the time, I believed it was okay because I did not gamble to excess, which was my version of The Big Lie. The truth was that I devoted too much time to gambling. It was time that should have gone toward job, family, and other important endeavors. While it wasn't robbing Peter to pay Paul, in it's own way, it was worse. Peter was robbed of money. A bookie was paid in cash, but there also was the cost to our humanity and dignity.

My bad habit started years before, in high school when I played poker with the guys on Saturday nights and later with members of my college basketball team. It evolved to occasional trips to Las Vegas, the first of which took place my sophomore year in college during spring break. It is amazing the places a fake ID can get you access. I learned to play craps, which was fun, though I can't say I ever was much good at it. I was just good enough to lose only the money I had budgeted, and how is that for logic? What type of person budgets money to lose?

After I graduated from college and began teaching, there were more trips to Vegas, and sports betting became greater parts of my routine. My first teaching job was at a Catholic high school on the South Side of Chicago that, because the teaching salaries were low, had a revolving door of staff. Out with those who could move onto something higher paying, and in with those in need of a job. Many rookie teachers cut their professional teeth at this school, which also was incubator for gamblers because the older teachers who hung on there all had side gigs and scams going. I learned things I never knew existed when participating in all of the betting pools and venturing to the race track with older members of the staff. There was a tradition of a big poker game the day before Thanksgiving break began. Not after school: the game cranked up first thing in the morning in the faculty lounge during that last day of classes. Both female and male members of the staff participated. Teachers would sit in during their prep and lunch periods. They employed student runners to deliver poker hands and carry bets to and from them during their classes. Lucky was the student who was the runner to a teacher on a hot streak. He received a nice tip. Woe was the kid who delivered bad news. He was considered bad luck and replaced.

After one year on the job, out the revolving door I went when I was hired at Bill O'Reilly High School, a much more professional place. At the Catholic High School, we gambled openly. At B.O. High, vices and improprieties were kept under wraps. Not long after I settled in at B.O., and hungry for a little action, I asked around and discovered no one was operating betting pools. The previous operator retired at the conclusion of the previous school year. "Would I be interested in running some pools?" I was asked.

Perhaps the oldtimer who inquired knew my last job was at a Catholic High School in Chicago.

I instituted a football, a basketball tournament pool, and a baseball pool. I was discreet, of course. Business was not transacted openly. Nothing was be posted on bulletin boards. Payouts were made on the QT. The first year, there were thirty players every week. Every year thereafter, there were at least one hundred. Among the participants were the man who was school principal when I was hired, the athletic director, and his secretary.

I made up the lists of college and pro teams, distributed them, collected the entries and fees, scored the entries, published the results, and paid out. I enjoyed being in on the action so much that I did not charge a fee or take a cut. Perhaps I was not the sharpest knife in the drawer. I should have taken something for all of the work I did. The least-favorite part of a teacher's job is grading papers, and I was correcting at least one hundred extra papers per week during football and basketball in addition to handling the money.

It was a built-in something to do. I desired to gamble, and I could do so against my fellow faculty members. It was the desire to be in on action, which I was not cognizant of at first. One of my co-workers, an oldtimer who'd just won a pool, in attempting to tip me, tipped me off. I refused to take the gratuity. He remarked, "Kid, I don't know why you do all of this if you don't take a kick back."

I joked, "It gives me something to do."

His retort was the payoff. "The only thing worse than losing is not being in on the action."

The remark was funny, but its value didn't hit me until much later. The old bird had provided an education, but like my future co-worker, I was oblivious. How could I immediately get Orpheus and Uterus but not that?

After a few years, some guys on the staff asked me if I would take their sports bets. Well, I didn't cover bets, but I knew of someone who did. So I took their action and laid it off to the guy. There weren't any problems. Except being the go-between is the same as being the bookie. So one day there was a problem.

An assistant principal, a humorless man in his first year in administration, summoned me. I thought it was to begin the process of my annual teacher evaluation, a nuisance in the form of a contractual formality. After I sat down, however, he informed me he had received evidence that I was conducting a bookmaking operation at school. He said he had received reports, and if the evidence held up, I would be fired.

He asked me if I ran sports betting pools in school.

He asked me if I took sports bets from staff members.

He asked me if money every changed hands in any of the related transactions.

Both of us knew all of the accusations were true. Everyone at B.O. knew it was true. I gave him my best Captain Renault impression and expressed shock. I did admit to one thing, but this was to myself, not to the assistant principal.

I regretted being caught.

The assistant principal glared at me. He informed me of two options, the first of which was to stick to my guns, deny the charges, and fight them. He added assuredly that he had sufficient evidence against me, that I would be fired, and the state's attorney would be contacted, after which I would be charged with gambling, from which there could be collateral damage related to the charges. He asked if I was aware a felony conviction could result in me losing my teacher pension.

If there is one thing that terrifies a teacher like no other, it is the thought of losing his or her pension, especially in in Illinois, where state and county politicians, in creating golden parachutes for themselves, had to include all government employees. Illinois pensions are among the most generous public pensions in America. Beyond the scary thought of losing my pension, there also was the embarrassment of being charged with a crime, and, whether exonerated or convicted, of securing another teaching position. Once your name appeared in the media, landing another job would become improbable.

Plus my parents would learn of it. Ouch.

The second option was for me to resign my teaching and coaching position. If I did so, I would walk out the door without charges, without anything going in my personnel file, and with a brief letter of recommendation. Nothing would appear in the media. I could pursue another teaching position because there would be no stink from B.O.

I asked the assistant principal if I could take a day to think about it. He said no, and he reached inside his desk and removed two letters, each of which he slid across his desk at me. One was a letter of resignation he had drafted for me. It had no mention of any wrongdoing, only that I had resigned. My name was printed at the bottom. The other letter was a brief letter of recommendation. His name was at the bottom, and his signature was on it.

He looked at me coldly and said, "You can sign and walk out, or I can pick up the phone and call the state's attorney."

I signed. After I did, he warned me that I had thirty minutes to pack all personal possessions and be off of school grounds. "I won't have security walk you out. That would be embarrassing. If I do not see you exit the front door and drive away within those thirty minutes, I will have security track you down and escort you out."

A cardboard box of books, papers, and other miscellaneous items in hand and hoping none of my now former colleagues would see me, I sneaked out a side door of B.O. High twenty minutes later. As I drove away, it hit me. My co-worker had been right. To me, only thing worse that losing was not being in on the action. Can you imagine? I was not immediately concerned because I no longer had money coming in, which was losing defined. What I thought about as I walked out the front door of B.O. High for the last time was that I would not have anything to do all day.

Chapter 4
Quicksand

Reality did not immediately sink in. Because I was disoriented, my parallel motivations were to find a way to generate some income while presenting to anyone to whom it might have mattered the illusion that I remained employed. An English teacher would call that logical fallacy. I was a history teacher. What had Santayana said?

Yes, at that time, yours truly the self-proclaimed logical thinker actually believed that illusion was as important as income. One of the reasons was my family. I came from a family in which everyone had a work ethic, and everyone strove for and achieved some measure of success in their careers. We earned good livings, owned houses in solid neighborhoods, and drove middle class status (i.e. practical) vehicles. Now back to the illusion I had to create. Because I resided in a state far away, fooling them for a while might be easy because the ruse would be by long distance. During my annual holiday visit, as long as they didn't notice anything in my demeanor, I might pull it off.

Thus upon returning home for Christmas, the defrocked professional educator presented his best phony demeanor. I laughed and reminisced with everyone. I congratulated everyone for the positive changes in their lives, remained silent as long as I could, and, when pressed, I fibbed about my career. (Sigh) My parents were good people who raised us right. At that time, my mom and dad still worked, but they had begun to openly discuss retirement and where they might relocate. One of my brothers, who'd just earned a promotion at work, was engaged. A sister who was a few years younger was expecting. It would be the first for her and her husband. An older sister and her husband had two children, and it gave me joy to see their children and play with them. During Christmas dinner, I was asked how soon I would be head of the history department. "Oh, it won't be too much longer," I lied with a smile. "Would someone mind passing the mashed potatoes?"

I could not help but feel happy for every member of my family. Why did I also feel as though I had grown apart from them? Or was it because I hadn't been honest with them and was felt like the failure of the family? Whatever the psychology, it very much bothered me.

Signs of the failure that had crept into my routine, by the way. During my visit, I ate too much and slept too late in my old bedroom. What helped was that my competitive family – not gamblers, but competitors – played games at night. You name it, we played it, and not for funzies. Charades, cards, board games. It was good to see my mom wrinkle her nose at a play that went against her, one of my sisters punch one of us in the shoulder in mock anger or enthusiastically hug one of us, and hear my dad say, "What the bloody heck!" For the record, my dad is not British.

Yep. I'm bragging about what transpired with my family. The visit may have saved me from getting into quicksand. I always had been possessed by the belief that if I devoted myself full time to gambling I could make a living at it. Distractions such as teaching and coaching jobs simply had not enabled me to give gambling the attention it truly deserved were part of that fallacy. Before the visit, I mistakenly believed I was on the hot seat to turn my belief into reality. Afterward, I was more grounded. I had regained some confidence. Was I going to gamble to pick up a few bucks? Yes. Would I go all in? No. Quicksand did not appeal to me.

Not that I wasn't tempted to jump in with both feet. The bookie to whom I'd been laying off my B.O. bets was a guy named Jimmy. I am not sure why, but I suspected he might be easy pickings. Why is it that we automatically assume that if someone doesn't possess the same level of education we have attained, or if they're in an alternative occupation, they are inferior to us? When we enter their realms, the arenas where they have expertise and are comfortable, don't we concede to them the home field advantage?

I smile about it now. Back alleys, the netherworld, hell? Oh, yes. For those who reside there, they are home field advantages.

Chapter 5
Jimmy

According to those who frequented his bar and placed bets with him, Jimmy the bookie was "a fat, smelly boozehound who seemed to be experiencing the onset of paranoid schizophrenia." A disgruntled gambler once pointed a finger at Jimmy where he sat across the bar and whispered to me, "Watch out for him. He'll gut you for a nickel." There were rumors that Jimmy had murdered someone, that he was a member of organized crime, that he had been married but his wife vanished never to be heard from again, and that he had embezzled millions of dollars from a former employer. To date, none of the aforementioned have been verified. They are mentioned to illustrate some points, not to earn any.

When people fail or are in the process of failure, they tend to affix blame elsewhere, denigrate someone, or attempt make someone else look bad. It makes the person at fault look better, or so they believe. Humans enjoy stomping sour grape and serving the bitter product.

As this truism pertains to yours truly, Jimmy was my adversary. Flawed and untrustworthy as he was, however, he was not the precipitator of any of my issues. The poisonous root in my lifestyle was bad decision making. Jimmy was the fertilizer which helped that root grow. Years later, I still wonder whether psychologically I was out to punish myself.

As for Jimmy, who was more interesting and less complicated than my psychology, of all the things he was or wasn't and no matter what anyone said about him, Jimmy was transparent. He was a simple read and completely understandable. Cue Fitz & The Tantrums. Jimmy was the biggest moneygrabber you ever could meet. He was worse than a college basketball coach and as twisted as a Cook County politician. Because of this – not merely a flaw but a complete lack of character —

everyone who ever dealt with Jimmy should have known exactly where they stood with him.

"How do you know you're in the wrong place?" I once heard a guy say. "Jimmy's there."

Among the many reasons the quote was true: to Jimmy, greed wasn't merely good. He proclaimed it to be a quality. When asked if he ever felt remorse about taking people's hard-earned money, Jimmy replied, "Somebody's gonna get it. Might'z well be me."

Cash was the fuel that kept Jimmy's engine running. It was the chip which powered his little calculator of a brain and his fast-counting fingers. In Jimmy's world, everything but the acquisition of money was a diversion, no matter how sick or disgusting those side trips might be. So it didn't matter if Jimmy drank so much late into a football Saturday or Sunday that he passed out. The next day, Jimmy would be a fanny kicker on the phone, abstaining from alcohol until the sun set and there were no more calls.

Jimmy got his start in the world of business early. As a younger man he decided to pass on college and go to work right out of high school. He was employed by a beer distributor and worked on a beer truck. For two years, Jimmy actually performed physical labor, and that was long enough for him to determine that he hated it. Eventually he used a political connection to land a job with what used to be known as "the phone company." This was in the era referred to as "B.C:" Before Cellular and prior to all of the mergers, acquisitions, and spinoffs. In those days there was just one phone company, and was a decent one.

That was "BJ:" Before Jimmy.

Employment with the phone company often was political in nature, and the hires knew when they came aboard, they were there to achieve goals set by their bosses. It didn't matter if they slacked off, lied, were hungover on the job, or stole. As long as their jobs got done, and they did not displease their bosses, they kept their jobs, climbed the corporate ladder, eventually became the bosses, were able to purchase what would prove to be very valuable stock, and retired well-to-do.

In *Master of the Senate* by Robert Caro, a White house reporter is quoted as saying, "When Lyndon Johnson was elected president, that office changed forever." So it was when Jimmy went to work at the phone company. The comparison is a stretch, but it applies. Hey, I'm a history teacher. We love appropriate historical quotes. If your phone service wasn't enough to snuff during the time Jimmy was an employee, well, Jimmy and his ilk didn't have the best skills. Or work ethic. Or attendance. This may have been why Jimmy eventually was "assigned" - no one within the phone company ever was demoted or retrained - to payphone collection. In that role, Jimmy drove a company vehicle on a designated route and emptied the coin boxes of payphones. According to a former phone company executive who lived in my neighborhood, the only division of the phone company that reported a steady decline in revenue during that era was payphones.

Jimmy developed his taste for booze and an aversion to humanity during the phone company phase of his life, and he must have found himself without any substantive interests though lots of time and money on his hands. That was when Jimmy fell in with the wrong crowd and began to gamble seriously. As time passed and Jimmy became – well, let's just say he became less appealing to the mainstream - his social circle became similarly less attractive. Friday nights lasted until work on Monday mornings as Jimmy whored, gambled, and drank himself into a stupor on a regular basis.

Then something transformational happened. Consider it an epiphany if such a term can be applied to Jimmy. He bought a bar and became the wrong crowd. At age thirty-five and with a healthy bank balance, Jimmy acquired what had been a corner saloon. It had an inherited clientele and a private backroom where business could be conducted discreetly. The bar was perfect for Jimmy. Yet reportedly there was one challenging detail: a name for the new joint. Jimmy believed it required a moniker that would reflect a certain ambiance and indicate his stature. After some soul searching, Jimmy came up with the perfect name: Jimmy's.

The new proprietor required no assistance bringing in entertainment. That circus was provided by Jimmy himself and his customers.

Nobody ever knew what was going to happen at Jimmy's, but many showed up to participate. The tone was set the first night he owned the joint. There was a bloody fight during which one of the combatants had a portion of his lower lip bitten off. Jimmy decided that this was better than Monday Night Football, and he looked into the possibility of having fighting (not to be confused with the sport of boxing) at the bar. What Jimmy proposed was a precursor to mixed martial arts and the alternative types of barbaric competitions popular today, but Cook County nixed the idea. You know a moneymaking idea is bad if Cook County won't approve it. Yet Jimmy, as he usually did, made out anyway. He simply decided to rely on the impromptu fights that sometimes broke out, during which patrons learned to stand clear and enjoy the action. Jimmy always bought drinks for the combatants, even when they had to be transported to the hospital, Their booze was poured into a little red plastic cup and off they went.

According to legend, this was how the cargo cup was invented.

Occasionally Jimmy got some exercise and participated in the fisticuffs. Late one Sunday evening, Jimmy and a few regulars were sitting at the bar drinking and watching a West Coast baseball game. Also at the bar was in irregular. He was young and college educated. He had long hair. He was glib, and he had a personality. It was these last two which did him in.

The irregular and one of the regulars got to talking about the baseball game, and the conversation escalated into a difference of opinion. Things went from trash talk to physical after the regular called the irregular "college boy."

At first, it was a fair fight. This didn't go at Jimmy's. Other regulars jumped in. So did Jimmy. They punched, kicked, and stopped the irregular around the bar and into submission. After they were finished, Jimmy opened the door, and they threw him into the street. The victors returned to their bar stools and resumed drinking.

Someone must have called the cops. It wouldn't have been anyone from Jimmy's. That would have gotten a regular a lifetime ban. Or worse. What happened at Jimmy's did not necessarily stay at Jimmy's, but it was settled at Jimmy's. Speculation was the victim crawled to a pay phone. Anyway, the front door of Jimmy's swung open, a uniformed officer stood in the doorway, and he looked around. At the sound of the door opening, everyone at the bar turned to look. It was a cop. So what? They turned back.

When the officer announced, "Is there a problem here?" no one responded. Why would they? There wasn't a problem. Yet as though on cue, the bruised and bloodied irregular crawled on his knees and elbows to the open door. With all of his strength, he raised a hand, pointed a finger at the men at the bar, and rasped. "Those are the ones, officer. They are the ones who beat me."

The cop turned his stare from the men at the bar to the man below him. With distain, he told him, "You'd better crawl away from here before I beat you." He let the door close on the victim and stepped up to the bar. He took off his hat and set it upside down on the bar. The bartender poured him a draft and set it before him. While he was enjoying a beer on the house, Jimmy rose from his stool, walked over to the cash register, removed an envelope, and placed it in the hat. When the cop was done with his beer, he put the hat on and walked out.

The police weren't always so courteous. One Saturday afternoon at Jimmy's, the bartender, a holdover from previous ownership, refused to refill the glass of a Chicago cop named Marty who was on duty, in uniform, and overserved. To the dismay of patrons, the drunken officer pulled his service revolver and stuck it in the bartender's nose, ensuring himself one more drink.

"What da hell is wrong with Marty?" one bar regular whispered to another.

"Yeah. What da hell's he thinkin'?" the guy next to him agreed. "Wid dat kinda leveridge, he coulda ordered a roun' on da house."

The bartender was the smart one. He fled, never to return.

On the opening day of Major League Baseball one year, a conga line of fans led by Jimmy's accordion playing Uncle Bob snaked their way into and throughout the bar, then had a raucous all night celebration after their charter bus returned from a White Sox victory. This in itself wouldn't have been unusual, but the bus trip originated from another bar, and the drunken group wanted post-game action the sponsoring bar could not provide. Instead of returning to that bar, exiting the bus, and driving their cars to Jimmy's, the loyal White Sox and Jimmy's fans booted out the owner in front of his own tavern and commandeered the bus, perpetrating what may have been the one and only bus hijacking led by a drunken accordion player in White Sox Opening Day history. As Casey Stengel once said, though not about Jimmy's, "You could look it up."

Jimmy himself provided everything from shock to laughter to trends. Involved in a heated card game while standing at the end of the bar early one evening, Jimmy, never one to let exercise get in the way of anything, was desperate for a urinal. In full view of the crowded bar, the drunken Jimmy unzipped, unfurled, and urinated into a nearby garbage can. Those paying attention were astonished, which in itself was astonishing, though one regular put it in perspective when he remarked, "At least he did it during the shuffle."

Not long afterward, Jimmy reversed himself on bathroom protocol and made statements on cleanliness and competition in the process. During an evening when he did make it all the way to the men's room, Jimmy emerged with a scowl. "Can't anyone hit the damned bowl!" he growled in reference to the wet floor in the men's room. The outburst not only served to improve lavatory hygiene, it also inspired the first annual "Jimmy's Accuracy and Long Distance Shootout," a peeing contest held in the yard behind the bar. Jimmy competed and finished first in accuracy and third in the distance competition.

Jimmy also proved that he had the habits of his patrons in mind, though certainly not their health, when he installed a smoker's lounge in the bar. The surprise was that it was one of the few things he did legally. Jimmy had built onto the back of the bar a large room that he had designated a public area. It was not part of the bar proper. This meant patrons who entered the room were not required to observe county or local smoking ordinances, which mandated that it was illegal to smoke in public businesses such as bars and restaurants. Jimmy called his smoker's lounge "The Amenity." He had a sign installed above the entrance to it. There were no tables or bar stools in The Amenity. The only creature comfort was the ledge installed along the walls for patrons to set drinks and ash trays. Because "amenities ain't free," as Jimmy reminded customers, Jimmy offered for sale tobacco products and smoking devices.

Gambling was the real lure of Jimmy's, of course, and the big man offered every kind of action imaginable. If a bettor wanted action on the day's sporting events, Jimmy covered wagers on everything that had odds, a point total, or a point spread. All a patron had to do was approach him at his "office," which is what he called his stool at the far corner of the bar. Events involving Chicago teams? Jimmy either had squares and as many zero-to-9 pools as it took to satisfy the customers. Liked to gamble but preferred to bet on things other than sports? There was always some type of card game, liar's poker, or the "shake of the day," in which for a fee, a customer was handed five dice in a leather cup. He or she was required to shake the cup and roll out all five. If they displayed the same number, they won. "Shake of the day" was a popular game because the pot accumulated rapidly and a player had a chance at big money for a small price. The pot at Jimmy's often went into the thousands of dollars before a patron was able to produce five of a kind in a single roll.

Not that all of the action at Jimmy's was sedentary or emanated from a bodily function. Jimmy had regulation horseshoe pits installed in the patio behind the bar and organized a horse shoe league comprised of teams from his bar and others in the area. During the winter, a dart league competed at Jimmy's three times per week. There was a winner—take—all pool tournament every other month. All of the activities featured a buy-in and a lesser payout because Jimmy got a cut of everything.

For those who didn't mind spending really big bucks to be involved, Jimmy had just the thing. He outdid himself by coming up with the disaster/catastrophe pool for all professional sports. For a one thousand dollar entry fee, a bettor could enter Jimmy's sick world of sports. All he needed to have was the first unlucky sports team to be wiped out in a plane crash, bus accident, hotel fire, earthquake, or any other disaster or catastrophe.

Jimmy had a printed computer list of each professional sports team, the weeks of the year, and the name of each participant. For five thousand dollars, participants rotated teams each week throughout the calendar year regardless of sporting season. If a team was wiped out during the week you had them, you were a winner.

Of course, one week you may have had a team which wasn't in season. This meant you weren't likely to win unless individual players were stalked by snipers, there was a salmonella outbreak at a team party, or a group of jealous wives and girlfriends found out what professional athletes actually had been doing on the road all these years and hired hit men. Any of those things could happen in Jimmy's twisted imagination.

There were a few additional rules. At least seventy—five per cent of a team had to meet its doom. Managers, coaches, and clubhouse personnel didn't count. Pandemics did not pay out. Asked why by a patron, Jimmy's snapped, "Becuz a da Chinese!"

Jimmy hated China and all things China years before it became en vogue for conservative Republicans. Yet he loved Russia. Informed by a patron that China and Russia were allies, Jimmy scoffed, "Yeah, right. Dat's what Putin wans everybody ta think." Jimmy and Putin? For quite a while after Jimmy's statement, bar regulars discussed the possibility of a Russian missile "accidentally" downing a team's charter flight, and since that time there have been rumors that the leading conspiracy theorists who would cause great chaos in future eras all got their starts at Jimmy's.

Ethnic biases, geopolitical alliances, and conspiracy incubators aside; if the Disaster Pool did not have a winner during the calendar year, the money rolled over into the next year, at which time participants had to cough up an additional thousand for the privilege of being in the pool again. Jimmy himself kept the money in an interest bearing account and pocketed the interest as juice on the action. He also resold, at full value plus ten per cent, spots not claimed by previous participants, and pocketed the overage.

"A guy's gotta make a livin'!" is what Jimmy growled to complainers. Getting a cut of everything ensured that Jimmy supplemented his already very good living.

A dozen years into the bar and illegal gambling business, a surprising thing happened. Jimmy was fired from his job with the phone company. While not significant from an HR standpoint - an employee had to be a certified loser to be released by the phone company, and Jimmy qualified - the surprise was that it took management so many years to realize Jimmy should go. By no coincidence, Jimmy's departure precipitated a spike in payphone revenue the likes of which the phone company never had experienced.

While Jimmy no longer enjoyed the salary and benefits of a corporate employee, the bar business and his bookmaking operation were quite lucrative. There also was a rumor that Jimmy had another side business, something outside of the bar and on a large scale. No one seemed to know what it was or whether such an enterprise actually existed, however. Either way, Jimmy had made a smooth transition to the booze and bookmaking businesses full time as he beat a great many suckers out of serious money.

Yes, there always were suckers who walked into the bar with the absurd idea that they were going to beat Jimmy out of serious money. I know this because for a brief while I was one of them.

Chapter 6
Or So I Thought

Had 1 really been paying attention, I never would have bet with Jimmy or spent any time at his bar. Like Jimmy, I was in transition, and my transition caused me to be detached from the mainstream. When we don't go to work each day, when we don't see quality people and interact with them in personal and professional situations, we lose not only a connection but an understanding of them. We fail to notice cultural and political changes. We lose perspective. It becomes difficult to identify with others and to empathize with them. I never thought about any of the interpersonal and socio-emotional consequences. I didn't dream I could suffer the same fate as so many other unemployed schmucks or even worse, join all those broke and battered gamblers who'd hit rock bottom. I was too educated and too smart to become unaware, and I was too good and too lucky to be beaten, especially by a loser like Jimmy. It would in fact be a pleasure beating him, a triumph or good over evil, so to speak.

Or so I thought.

Chapter 7
Dis 'n Dat

Merry Christmas to me. I'd been terminated by B.O. High a few weeks before Christmas, and I began my full-time assault on Jimmy at the perfect time, if there was such a thing as a perfect time to gamble. With college football playing bowl games and the NFL concluding its regular season and transitioning to the playoffs, football betting was prime. Try to stop flowers from blooming in the spring. I dare you.

I always believed it easier for the informed bettor to win on football at the end of the season because he or she has followed the teams all season and knows them well. The good teams are on cruise control. The dogs roll over. A bettor who zeroed in on a few teams instead of trying to play them all could make a killing. That's exactly what I did through New Year's Day, beating Jimmy out of twenty seven thousand dollars.

On settlement day at the bar, Jimmy surprised me little by playing the role of the gracious loser. Not gracious for a human, but gracious for Jimmy. I found him in his usual spot, on a stool in the darkest corner of the bar, and sat down next to him.

I was in an extremely good mood, and why wouldn't I be? "Are you buying, Jimmy?" I needled.

"You're up dis kinda dough, you can buy yer own beer," Jimmy growled. If you listened closely, you could interpret the tone of Jimmy's growls. This one was angry-hostile.

I signaled the bar tender for a draft. Jimmy had more to say, which I did not mind. It was his dime, many dimes actually, and they were going into my piggy bank.

The beer arrived. I raised the glass to Jimmy and took a sip. It tasted like the best beer I ever had. "How and where do we do this?" I asked Jimmy.

Jimmy grimaced. "When we do DIS (He raised his voice on the mispronounced word for emphasis.), we do it privately. We don't do NUTTIN' (more emphasis) public involving payouts. We go downstairs." Jimmy jerked his right thumb over his shoulder at a door behind him and stood up. "Finish your beer. Count your blessings. Walk downstairs, take a right, and opena first door."

"Because someone is waiting downstairs to crack me over the head with a blackjack?"

Finally! I elicited a smile from the big man. "Why?" Jimmy chuckle-growled. "You don' think yer gonna to be giving da money back ta me?" He rose from the stool, waddled across the room, and disappeared into the darkness of a doorway, and down the stairs.

While I finished my beer, I thought about what he said. It was a warning that made sense to a history teacher. I paused. It was my turn to insert emphasis. I WAS a history teacher. Past tense. As for a truism of gambling, every bettor who won and continued gambling lost the money back. They got stuck in gambling quicksand and lost more trying to win back what they lost."

The actor Mickey Rooney, a lifelong gambler, offered a telling quote. In his autobiography, he confessed, "I lost my first two dollar bet on a horserace when I was ten years old, and I've lost ten million dollars trying to win it back."

It wasn't Abraham Lincoln or Dr. King, but it was powerful, and it provided the first clear-headed thought I had about gambling since I got myself so out of control that it cost me my job. When I walked through that dark doorway and down the stairs, I did look over my shoulder for someone who might jump out at me. No matter what he said, it was Jimmy's. Being hit from behind with a blackjack went with the territory. Yet I arrived downstairs unscathed, followed a light that shone from inside a doorway, and stepped inside a room. Jimmy handed me an eight-and-a-half-by-eleven envelop. "Open it and count it," he said.

I looked at him. He told me to count the money, but the expression on his face told me not to do so. It was a moment, perhaps *the* moment, in our new business relationship. "No need," I told him.

Jimmy approved. He nodded, but he did not smile. "Take good care of my money."

I turned and walked out. As I walked up the stairs, out of the basement, and into the neon light of the bar, my head was on a swivel around for anyone who might want to separate me from the money. Outside in my car, I did count the money. All things considered, it still was Jimmy.

Chapter 8
The Corner of Cherry & Bliss

There are times of year when good teaching jobs were available. The holidays are not among them. The "windows," as they were known in education, opened late spring of each year and closed with the end of the school year before reopening when administrators returned from their vacations and made the last necessary, sometimes desperate, before schools re-opened.

There were exceptions if you had the right certification. A special education teacher could find a job at almost any time. It was estimated the largest cities in American always had hundreds of special ed openings. Math and science were areas that offered strong possibilities. My area, social studies, did not. I did check openings just in case, but the openings held true to form. It was unlikely I would find a teaching job until the windows re-opened in late spring.

I had to do something besides gamble. I hated to admit that Jimmy the heartless bookie was right. If I continued to gamble regularly, I would give him back all of the money and more. Then where would I be? That question produced was easy answers: looking over my shoulder for Jimmy's collector when I was late and could not pay. Scrounging. Wallowing in self-pity.

While a job for me in education was not available, the mainstream job market was good. I needed to work somewhere and make a few bucks until something substantial came along. I had seen and heard ads for Amazon jobs. I applied online, quickly was hired, completed onboarding, and went to work in an Amazon hub, as facilities were known, at Cherry and Bliss on the near northwest side of Chicago. The neighborhood was where Old Town ended, Bucktown began. The area was in transition from an aging warehouse district into rehabbed buildings with car dealerships, wholesalers, and lofts. If a company needed quantity space and had millions dollars to bring its concept to fruition, a dream became a reality.

Amazon scheduled its part-time workforce in four-hour and six-hour shifts. Workers booked shifts online on a first-come-first-served basis. The best shifts were gobbled up quickly. I didn't want to work eight to midnight. I was able to secure a few prime time shifts, however, because of the Amazon mandate that shift employees (those not hired to work full-time) were not permitted work forty-hour weeks. Amazon did not want to pay benefits and overtime to its employees. Only hub managers and other were full-time. "Associates" such as yours truly were considered part-time.

Aside from that, Jeff Bezos or whoever he hired to run Amazon got it when it came to human resources. When my employment began, I things continued to go smoothly than at any job I'd ever worked. When I clocked in and out, my work time was recorded for me. My online accounts allowed me to track hours. My pay quickly went into my checking account because all employees had direct deposit.

What I did not like and what nearly caused me to quit was that the job was boring. Walking around and around a warehouse was the most tedious thing I ever did.

Amazon pickers use hand scanner to find and select items for customer orders. When my scanner told me to go to Aisle G100-500 Slot 6 and pick a jar of peanut butter, I reported to that location, scanned the bar code on the shelf and the item, placed the item into a bag, whose label I also scanned so the cloud in which all of the information was stored knew I picked the item. When my order was complete, the scanner told me to go to "slam," which meant that I was to report to a conveyor with a computer, scan the label on my bag, print a label for it, and seal in onto the bag. Finally, I delivered my orders, bagged and labeled, to location at the front of the hub for a delivery driver to pick up. If my bag said G4, I found a shelf on a metal rack that was labeled G4, and placed the order there. Deliveries went out every two hours, and when each two-hour window neared close, there was a frenzy to slam orders and get them onto shelves. If all of the orders that were supposed to go out at 4 p.m., for example, did not, the discrepancy showed up on a manager's computer, and he or she became very upset. Managers were rated on accuracy and on-time delivery. Too many orders packed wrongly, delivered late, or not at all, and a manager was out of a job. It wasn't that someone had to have a book or a jar of peanut butter by 4 p.m. Because Jeff Bezos promised they would have it within two hours, his employees had to meet that deadline.

After picking for Amazon for two weeks, I was bored out of my mind. Working a late afternoon shift on a rainy Saturday (always a very busy day at the hub), I decided I had enough. When my four hours were up, I would walk away and not schedule additional shifts. Je suis fini! There were maybe ninety minutes remaining in my Amazon career when a supervisor named Donny stopped me in the aisle in which I was sleep walking and said, "The parking lot situation is screwed up. Would you mind going out there to direct traffic?"

Would I! I'd have done anything to get out of picking. Well, almost anything. It was raining and maybe 40 degrees. I didn't have weather gear, and that was what I told Donny.

"Oh, don't worry about that. We have waterproof coats, and there are gloves. We also have flashlights."

"Just show me where," I said, and just like that, I had found my niche in an early evening January drizzle in the Amazon parking lot. It was more than Cherry and Bliss. It was heaven. I loved directing traffic! I'm a people person, and I enjoyed interacting with the drivers. The issue was that the drivers liked to take shortcuts. They wanted to get in and out of that hub with their orders as fast as possible. Remember that two-hour window? Drivers had deadlines, too. They knew they were supposed to enter and leave via the driving lanes and park only in designated spots when arriving to pick up their orders, but they weren't doing so because cutting corners saved them valuable minutes.

You know how the trouble started. One driver bent the rules. Another saw him do so and did same. And the next driver. And the next. A driver would cut off another and an arguments ensued. Name calling and cursing followed. Occasionally punches were thrown. One driver pulled a gun, and that was what forced Donny to assign an associate to clean up Dodge. Of course, Donny didn't put it that way. He certainly did not mention a gun. I didn't learn of the gun incident until much later. Had I, I wouldn't have worked there. Rain gear is one thing. Bullet proof vests are another.

After the new sheriff arrived in the form of yours truly, the acrimony ended. My teaching experience helped. I played it like Andy of Mayberry. I directed drivers in and out of driving lanes and into parking spots. I set up oranges cones that were easy to follow. I was forceful but friendly, personable but fair. I helped drivers wheel carts full of orders, and I helped them load vehicles. I commiserated with them. "What do you need?" I would ask. The drivers appreciated that. Suddenly the parking lot was organized. It also was peaceful. My new tasks made me feel important. That first afternoon, I was supposed to leave at four, I stayed until 6:30. I would have stayed longer but I didn't have waterproof shoes, and my feet became wet and cold.

"Thanks so much," Donny told me when I re-entered the hub to log out, and that made me feel good, too.

"Does anyone have that job?"

"What job?"

"Directing traffic. Hauling carts."

"Directing traffic was a one-time thing. Usually the driver's don't get that out of hand. No one does carts. When we do, we just send out an associate."

"I'll do carts," I told him. "I'll take care of the entire parking lot."

Donny's expression was one of surprise, but he quickly said, "The job is yours."

Have you ever re-invented anything? That is what I began to do when I returned for my shift the next morning. Donny wasn't there. A manager named Betty was. After logging in, I approached her with trepidation. What if she wouldn't let me work the parking lot? I was not going back to picking.

Betty read my mind. "You're all set for the parking lot."

Donny must have given her a heads up. The waterproof shoes I was wearing did not touch the ground as I headed over to get the coat and gloves.

The drivers who picked up and delivered multiple orders every two hours sometimes arrived as much as thirty minutes before their scheduled pick up times. They entered the hub, located one of the sturdy plastic four-wheeled carts they needed, and, if the orders were ready, stacked their orders on the carts. They wheeled them down a ramp to the parking lot and their cars or vans. After they were loaded, they zoomed away. The empty carts remained where the driver's left them. The lot would be empty except for the carts and yours truly. I had to bring all of the carts back inside the hub, but that was not what concerned me. What if Betty told me to come back in and pick until the next delivery window opened? I needed to keep busy.

I began collecting the carts. It was similar to a cattle roundup except the carts didn't meander, right? Wrong. Carts were all over the parking lot. Sometimes they just waited for me. When the wind picked up, however, they would roll in every direction and down Bliss Street. I didn't have a lasso. I grabbed the handle of one, wheeled it into the back of the next, and then another to form a small train. I found that I could manipulate the last cart so that it steered all of them. It was linear transport. We didn't need to go around corners until we arrived at the entry door, but that was the easy part. Getting them to the door was the thing. I engineered my train up the ramp, swiveled the last one into an angle so it would not roll down the ramp, and ran to the front of the train and begin pushing carts into the hub.

That first day, my trains were three carts. Choo choo. Inside the hub they went, where I lined them into neat rows. Soon I wondered if I could push more. I lined up six, then eight. Choo Choo. No problem. Here we come. Ten. Chooooo! Still good. Twelve, fourteen. Make way for the cart train! It was a competition I had with myself, and on it rolled. Before I quit Amazon, I think I had lined up twenty-four carts and pushed them up the ramp. I could have done more – there were 30 carts - but the ramp wasn't long enough to hold more than twenty four carts.

I almost found a way around that, too. The carts were boxes on wheels. There was a handle in the rear, the top was walled square so the items would not slide off unless the drivers stacked them too high – which they occasionally did - and the bottom of the cart was same. The front wheels rotated in any direction the driver chose to steer.

Before long, I decided to stack the carts and form them into a double-decker train. I would lasso a cart (figuratively), pick one up, and stack it atop another. I'd pull another behind and another atop that. Soon I was pushing into the hub a double decker train of black carts. I'd achieved my goal. It was a new Cherry and Bliss Hub record. For all I knew it was an overall Amazon record. I had improvised and streamlined the process. I'd hustled. I felt great. Invigorated. Important. All I feelings I'd not had in a very long time. Since I had stopped teaching. The expressions on the faces of the supervisors, my co-workers, and the drivers indicated they felt something, too. The expressions said, "This guy is an innovator. He's making my job easier."

Before anyone knew it, the parking lot, cart location, and order pick up ran smoothly and efficiently. Okay, I didn't need to stack carts for things to be more efficient, but I was competing with myself, and it was fun. At first, all I wanted to do was beat the boredom. Now I wanted to get more than twenty four carts in one train back inside the hub. Because it was Amazon, however, something happened. As I was to learn during my time there, something always did.

I'd been master of the parking lot maybe two weeks. I was working a weekday late-morning-to-afternoon shift as well as some weekends, and that was another thing. Once the supervisors realized I was performing tasks no one else wanted, better shifts opened up for me. All of the managers wanted me to work for them. One morning, the big boss - the guy who ran the hub - arrived and walked through the parking lot toward the main entrance. "Good morning," he said to me with a smile. Apparently what I was doing made it all the way to the top. I noticed he eyeballed my stacked carts. Perhaps I would receive a commendation. Well, not exactly. An order quickly came down from the top. For safety reasons, no more stacking carts.

That didn't matter. I had more innovations up my sleeves. I wasn't picking. I was happy. There would be no stopping me, not for a while anyway. As I clocked out after one of my shifts, I noticed a single sheet of notebook paper tacked onto the bulletin board. Someone had started a poem. There was one stanza. It read.

We work at the corner of Cherry and Bliss.
A place, they tell us, Greek gods have kissed.
You need groceries or clothing?
Just send your list
To the corner of Cherry and Bliss.

Chapter 9
The Joy of Frugality

Hitting Jimmy for such a big score right out of the box could have been the worst thing that could have happened to me. Had it gone to my head, as it would have almost any other gambler, I might have figured I could not lose and began to gamble with impunity: i.e. out of control. Luckily, Jimmy scared me. It was not what he said. Okay, that scared me, too, as would any warning hiss of a snake. It was Jimmy himself who was alarming. Never had I known anyone like him, and I quickly sensed from our conversation that to trust him would be a grave mistake. Jimmy struck me as utterly ruthless, the type of individual capable of anything that would put money into his pocket.

There also was another factor, and it was more powerful than Jimmy. Both of my parents were frugal. When I was growing up, our family lived well, but our lifestyle was far from extravagant. There never was any waste of food or resources. When someone exited a room, the lights were turned off. We had no leaky faucets, and water was not allowed to run for it to become hot or cold. You didn't waste electricity. Water. Resources. Money! To do so was a sin. Growing up, when my siblings or I wanted or needed money, we heard one of two answers. "No!" or that alternative to flat out rejection, "Go to work for it." When we'd heard the latter enough times, we heeded the advice. My siblings and I learned the value of a buck and developed work ethics in the processes. We created businesses. We cut lawns and raked leaves, and we shoveled snow. People around the neighborhood knew that if they had a task they needed done, they could call one of us. For a small stipend, we were available.

Here is something we laughed about. When we graduated from college, entered the workforce, and received out first paychecks, each of us went out and purchased a big ticket item. The purchases varied. One sibling bought a stereo system. Another went on an exotic vacation. Mine was the purchase of a new car. After we did so, instead of experiencing the great joy of spending power, our reactions were the same: buyer's remorse. Why in the hell did I do that? Years later, sitting around reminiscing, we talked about it. We laughed. Everyone agreed. The purchases were acts of rebellion against our parents. The ensuing *Ah Ha* moments and our returns to frugality were reaffirmations of our parents.

I was the offspring of frugal parents, and that would never change. A twenty seven thousand dollar windfall was not to be squandered. At the time, I lived in a house in a near south suburb. I used some of the money to pay down my mortgage. I had some credit card debt. Nothing out of control, mind you, but it was debt. I made that disappear.

Unfortunately, life became more expensive the moment I was fired from my teaching job. This was before affordable care was offered by the federal government. For the unemployed, health care benefits and insurance were very expensive. When you were employed and didn't have a major medical expense, you did not know just how expensive they were because your employer paid some or all of your health care premiums. After I resigned from B.O., I received in the mail an offer to purchase the Cobra coverage that by law was offered to former employees. The name of the coverage was appropriate. The cost of that coverage is lethal. I needed coverage. I paid the high premiums.

Okay, I did continue to place bets with Jimmy, but I did so out of gambling etiquette or when absolutely necessary: i.e. a few of my former co-workers who'd participated in my pools and who occasionally made bets through me still wanted to bet. I covered their action. If their bets were too big for me, I laid them off on Jimmy. Occasionally, I bet a strong hunch.

There was one more very important factor. Quitting Jimmy after hitting him for a big score might not have been a good idea. What might he do, I wondered? Jimmy had to be connected on multiple levels. Were he not, he could not have continued to operate. A word from Jimmy, and someone would pay me a visit. I imagined the cops being tipped off to my gambling or a sinister figure waiting for me in my driveway after I returned from a shift at Amazon. As a different form of health care, I paid homage to Jimmy. I stayed healthy by continuing to bet with him, albeit judiciously.

Chapter 10
The One Thing Not Covered by Rule

Each day when I reported to the hub at Cherry and Bliss, I noticed there were piles of returned items. If someone placed an order, but no one was home when it arrived, it was returned. The rule was that on a vehicle delivery, someone had to be home to accept it.

To me that was an odd rule. If someone paid for it, leave it at their door. Yet there was an Amazon rule even odder, and this one I liked: any returned food item had to be disposed of in the dumpster behind the hub.

My hub had all manner of goods: perishables and non-perishables. It was a department store that everything from alarm clocks to zebra stuffed animals. Yet ii also sold food items. There were fresh and frozen fruits and vegetables and meats, bread and baked goods, cereal, milk, alcohol. On and on it went. It didn't take me long to figure out what Amazon was. Many of the managers had come from the grocery business or other aspects of retail. You've heard different expressions. If something is unusually big, it's on steroids. If something is very fast, it's on roller skates. Amazon was the grocery business on steroids on roller skates.

The returned items were left outside of the glass wall at the interior entrance of the hub. The managers were inside the glass. One always sat at a window so that she could talk to drivers and associates working outside of the glass such as yours truly. One day an associate named Kim said to me, "When you have a few minutes, get a cart and throw this stuff into the dumpster."

A delivery window had just closed. That always brought about a brief downtime for associates inside the hub until the next round of orders began coming in. I had to bring in my heard. After the carts were in, I could get rid of the returns.

"Okay," I told her.

There was a variety of items, some of which were perishables, and I had to make three trips. None of the food items had been opened. The frozen foods had not so much as begun to thaw because they were in Amazon freezer bags. All of the goods could have been returned to the shelves. I never learned the reason Amazon mandated all returned had to be disposed of, but I understood that loss due to this rule was great.

I stacked each delivery of perishables inside of the huge garage door. After I had everything, I pressed the button, and the door opened. The first thing I saw was the big green dumpster appear before me. To my right something was moving. People. Several men waited outside for door to open. At first, I believed the three men were homeless. In Chicago, it was common to see people dumpster dive. I soon realized, however, that while the men were shabby, their clothes were not ragged or filthy. Also, a pickup truck was parked nearby. The group of men had been tipped there were quality groceries free for the taking.

I told them, "You know I can't hand this stuff to you, right? I have to throw everything into the dumpster."

The oldest-looking member of the crew smiled and said to me, "No problem," and it wasn't. He turned and signaled another member of his group, and a man in coveralls climbed inside the dumpster. No sooner did the items land in the dumpster than he of them was inside handing it out to the others. A woman I hadn't noticed was standing at the back of truck, and they handed items to her. The process was made simple because the food was still in the delivery bags. They were having groceries delivered, but not to their door. It was to a dumpster, but the groceries were free.

I finished my disposal and pressed the button for the bay door to close. I returned to Kim and asked, "You know there are people out there taking what we throw out, right?'

She looked at me and shrugged her shoulders. Translation: there wasn't a rule about that. If there wasn't a rule, it wasn't a problem.

Amazon did have a rule that was a problem for many associates. Employees could not purchase items on duty and take them home. It was a subtle way of warning associates, "Thou shalt not steal." While I worked at Amazon, I noticed this rule was broken frequently during every shift. I would see associates discreetly munching on food items while working in the warehouse. I also noticed food and product wrappers, some in trash cans, but some on shelves where an associate had unpacked what they stole. Yet I never noticed anyone fired or so much as reprimanded for taking any items, and again, the loss to Amazon must have been great.

There also was a rule, relaxed long after I was gone, that associates could not have phones in their possession while on duty. The reasons for this were obvious: when people are on their phones, they tend not to focus on their work, and when they don't focus, mistakes are made. Some of the mistakes can lead to accidents. Employees often were fired for violating this rule. When someone was caught with their phone on duty, he or she received a warning to stow it in their locker and not bring it onto the floor (where work was done) during their shift. If they again were found in possession of their phone, they were terminated and escorted from the building by security.

During the time I was an Amazon employee, not once did I violate the phone rule. For a bettor, this was quite an accomplishment since those who gamble on games prefer to check scores in progress and phone in a recoup bets.

As for the theft rule, I lived by two that trumped it.

Waste not, want not. A man's gotta eat. Perhaps this was reflected in the second stanza of the poem on the bulletin board, which someone had added.

Oh, things are so perfect at Cherry and Bliss!

Our workplace is enchanted.
It is shrouded in mist.
The items we pick
The fairies have kissed
At the corner of Cherry and Bliss.

Chapter 11
Ed

Through the second weekend of February, I had done okay on my Super Bowl bets, but college and pro basketball were not kind to me. While I won, it wasn't anywhere near what I won from Jimmy the first time around.

Vital to me was that I had stuck to my game plan. I had done okay with my former co-workers, whose action I'd continue to take. When I believed one of my guys bet badly, I covered it, and I won more of these than I lost. As always, the very big bets were funneled to Jimmy, and a two of my guys had big winners. They were anxious for their money, so it was time to collect. There was some aggravation, however. I wound up having to go through Ed to get to Jimmy. Ed was Jimmy's roommate and flunky. He tended bar at Jimmy's.

To say that Ed was difficult to deal with would not accurately sum it up.

Of all the ways people described Ed, none were flattering, and most were interspersed with expletives. For reasons no one understood, Ed went out of his way to offend everyone. When Ed tended bar, he alternated between rudeness and ignoring the customers. He hated everyone except Jimmy, who he treated like a deity. Jimmy understood this, and he protected Ed. One day when a customer complained, Jimmy told him, "People come here ta drink or place a bet. Anybody looking fer ambulance should go to a fern bar." He inserted a profane gerund before fern bar for emphasis. No one informed Jimmy there hadn't been any fern bars since the 1970s, that he was wrong about customer service, or the correct term was *ambiance*. The balance sheet told Jimmy whether he was wrong or right. A guy sitting on a bar stool didn't.

When Jimmy was not available, Ed took the betting action that came in on the phone, and he was so rude on the phone that you wanted to strangle him. If a caller asked Ed if he got everything or to repeat the bets for accuracy, Ed would tell him or her, "Check your own bets, dumbass, and after you do, go diddle yourself."

Diddle is my euphemism. Ed preferred the explicitly vulgar term.

Like Jimmy, I knew of Ed from the old neighborhood. He was a few years older than Jimmy, which made him at least a dozen years older than me. Kids my age knew to avoid Ed because he didn't look or act right. He was a loaner who always wore all black. He smoked at an early age, cigarettes and marijuana, and occasionally he sniffed glue. Ed enjoyed picking on kids much younger and much smaller, but his favorite activity seemed to be lighting cats on fire. After dark, he walked the streets, entering unlocked cars to grab change or whatever he could steal for cigarette and weed money.

Ed did a stretch in juvie at 16, but it didn't straighten him out. After he returned home, Ed was too angry to finish high school. He dropped out. At 18, Ed's parents told him he had to move out of their home. He enlisted in the army, served a four-year hitch, but he did not rise above the rank of private, which wasn't easy, but in Ed's case was understandable. In the army, soldiers were promoted not for skills or intellect but for not screwing up and for getting along.

After returning home, Ed got a job with the local park district picking up trash in the summer and clearing snow in the winter. He bummed around sleeping on people's couches for as long as they could stand him. Weird and angry are not endearing. At the same time, Jimmy was the number two man on a beer delivery truck, and he was living in an apartment. He and Ed frequented the bar that would become Jimmy's. Because Jimmy was so cheap was why Jimmy and Ed became roommates. To Jimmy, money overcame character flaws. Ed was income. Later, when Jimmy bought a house, Ed went along.

As Jimmy became more prosperous, a few years after he'd joined the phone company, Ed became Jimmy's gopher. Whatever Jimmy didn't feel like doing - pretty much everything except gambling, drinking, and eating – fell to Ed: grocery shopping, housekeeping, errands, answering the phone, anything mean or ornery. When Jimmy bought the bar, Ed began to hang out there. One day, when a bartender didn't show up, Ed slid behind the bar. Eventually he quit his park district job and did whatever Jimmy needed him to do there, too. Much of it seemed to be standing and hate-staring at whoever walked into the bar.

Which was what he was doing when I walked in late one afternoon after my shift at Amazon. Ed was at the end of the bar opposite to where I sat down, but he didn't move. Instead he stood there arms folded across his chest and glared at me. How could Jimmy not know this was bad for business? A customer practically had to beg Ed for a drink. I politely waved my right hand, and I am certain Ed saw the gesture. Yet he refused move. I had to give Ed some respect. I smiled, nodded, and signaled again. All was done politely on my part, after which Ed moved in my direction very slowly as though he really didn't want to because he didn't.

Ed stood in front of me and shot me a disgusted look. Screw him. He did it to me. I would do it to him. Let him hang there awhile. Finally he said, "You gonna order a drink er pay rent onnat stool?"

"Bring me a draft," I said.

Ed smirked and shook his head before slowly walking to the tapper, holding a glass under it at an angle, and pulling a lever. He slowly walked back, tossed a cardboard coaster in front of me, and set the glass on it hard enough so that beer and foam ran down the outside of it. I tossed some bills on the bar where the beer and foam had run off of the coaster. That caused Ed to stand there and shoot me a dirty look. Hands on the bar, he sneered but said nothing. I suspected he was waiting to find out how far I would take it.

Ed didn't get that satisfaction from me. I waited a few moments and took a sip of my beer before informing him, "I'm here to see Jimmy."

Ed's chest heaved once. It must have released just enough of his hostility because he said, "Well, why didnya say so, loser?" He slowly swiveled around, picked up the receiver from a phone, and pressed a button. After a few seconds, he said, "Loser here ta see ya. Send 'im down?"

Ed hung up, swiveled back to me, and shot me a warning look. He had a menacing look for every situation. "You can go on down, but doan' try nothin' funny."

I was amused, not surprised. "Something funnier than what you just said?"

Ed pointed a boney, yellowish forefinger at me. The finger nail was dirty. It appeared to be more talon than human digit. "I remember ya. You're that real straight kid from the neighborhood. Straight but a smartass. You may have Jimmy fooled, but ya ain't got me fooled. I'm keepin' my eyes on ya."

My response was another long sip of my beer. I finished half of the glass before I swiveled off of the stool and headed across the room, through the dark doorway, down the stairs and back into the netherworld that contained Jimmy's headquarters. The area was dimly lit, and my eyes had difficulty adjusting, but I navigated the stairs and found the door. After I knocked, I heard a growl that sounded like, "It ain't locked."

Jimmy was seated at a large desk. On it were stacks of cash. Jimmy's fingers were counting rapidly. He didn't bother to look up. I was mesmerized by all of the money.

Jimmy growled, "Well?

I didn't know what to say and blurted out, "That's some personality Ed has. Am I correct he never has won an award for bartending?"

Not taking his eyes off of the money, still counting rapidly, he told me, "Every two weeks he gets 'n award. It's called a paycheck."

It wasn't worth it to respond further, and the volume of cash still was a distraction. Jimmy read my mind and asked over his shoulder, "You never seen dis much money before, have ya?" He laugh-growled.

His remark and cavalier attitude told me it was okay to stare, and I did. The bills were hundreds, fifties, and twenties. There were no tens, fives or singles. As for his fingers, I'd never seen appendages move so quickly. It was as though Jimmy's sausage-shaped digits were entities with minds of their own. When his fingers determined each stack had the right amount, they moved it to the side and began another.

I didn't dwell on his counting skills. Seeing all of that cash caused triggered a thought. To this day, I am surprised I asked what I was thinking.

"Does it ever bother you, Jimmy?"

"Does what bother me?" He harrumph-growled before asking and answering his own question. "Havin' ta count a lotta money? Nah. Not as long as I get ta keep it." Another chuckle-growl followed. He still had not looked at me.

"Taking people's hard-earned money in exchange for . . ." I had the idea, but I hadn't formulated it long enough to complete thought. Jimmy helped me.

"For helpin' people lose dere souls?" He said it so casually. Jimmy's head was down, but I suspected there was a smile on his face.

"Yes."

"Why should it?"

Finally I had formed the complete thought and said, "Because it's more than money. It's their lives, their pride, their dignity. You indulge them. You contribute to their . . ."

I could have finished it, but Jimmy was quicker. He'd been asked the question before.

"Destruction?" he asked without a shred of emotion.

"Yes," I said again. Later I realized that everyone who'd ever been in the bar, liquor sales, or gambling businesses either heard the question or asked it of themselves. To remain in the business, they needed to develop thick skins.

Jimmy looked up. For the first time in all the years I'd known him, he looked and sounded philosophical when he replied, "Da guys sittin' on bar stools upstairs wanna be somewhere, okay? Dey needa place ta unwind and be dere real selves. It's like dey wanna fit in somewhere, but dey don't know howta belong to a club or organization. At Jimmy's, ya come in and siddown. Boom! Just like dat, you're a member. Ya wanna drink? Okay. Ya wanna gamble? We got it for ya. Here ya go. Yer a member of da Jimmy's Family."

"It's a dysfunctional family," I told him.

"Dey chose it. Nobody put a gun ta dere heads."

I argued, "It's the same result. They drink, and they gamble. In some cases out of control. You provide the machinery. It's not a gun, but a different type of weapon of self-destruction."

Jimmy stunned me with his accuracy when he said, "You come here, college boy. What about dat? All doze years a ejacashun, and you still gotta come here. What I provide must not be too bad."

"I keep it under control."

"Boom! My job is to provide services. Your job is ta keep it under control. I res' my case."

Touche. He had me. Except I would not let it go. I had to be right even though I already had lost the argument.

"I do because I can."

"Again, not my problem. If they don't drink and gamble here, they're gonna go somewhere else. Somebody's gonna get dere dough. Might as well be me."

There it was again. The philosophy of crooks, gamblers, and so many politicians. Jimmy read my mind and added.

"So it ain't da Boy Scout oath. An' by da way, da Scouts have had problems dat go way beyon' money," Jimmy explained. "Inna real world, da code I live by woiks, an' everybody in my world understands it and lives by it. You think guys upstairs don' wanna beat my brains out? They wouldn' care if dey got my last nickel, an' I ended up livin' onna street."

I was disappointed, more with myself than Jimmy. I turned to leave. The big man stopped me.

"Wait," he instructed me. "Ya forgot dis."

When I turned back, he was holding out an envelope. It contained the winnings I had neglected to collect as well as a moment of truth. I accepted the envelope.

His head down, Jimmy's fingers resumed counting the bills. "Love ya', kid," he growled without looking up at me. "Stop by any time, an' don' take nuttin' fer granite."

For granted? It was funny, and the malapropism made me think of my former colleague, The Chihuahua. I hadn't thought of her in a while, and I wondered what became of her.

Chapter 12
Gaylord

"Go in the back and get a gaylord," Donny told me.

Gaylord was term Amazon had given the large box used for storage and disposal. A gaylord was approximately five feet long and four feet wide and seven feet high. Anyone who's ever had a refrigerator delivered knows what the box looks like, except Amazon's specially-made boxes are taller. There were stacks of gaylord lying flat on pallets throughout the warehouse. All an employee need to do was grab one and unfurl it, a process that occurred whenever Amazon needed to dispose of or move something in quantity. The something was thrown into a gaylord.

That day, the order was to collect all vinyl cold storage bags and throw them into a gaylord. Previously, when a customer ordered a cold or frozen item, it was placed in one of those insulated bags. The customer kept the bag until her or his next delivery, at which time the drivers picked up the cold storage bag and returned it to the hub to be re-used. Ever-calculating Amazon determined those cold bags were cost inefficient, and it would not continue to use them. The order came down from high. *From this day, cold or frozen items shall be placed inside of plain paper bags with the other grocery items.*

Amen.

After the drivers received the order, they began returning the bags. When they walked into the hub, they threw them into a pile near the entrance. Hundreds of bags piled up. My job, besides the parking lot and the carts, was to get all of the bags into gaylords. Plural. That gaylord was the first of many I would get for that purpose, and throwing cold storage bags inside of them was in addition to my other tasks and innovations such as ensuring orders were on the proper racks so that drivers could find them and doing anything else I could to help the drivers get their carts full of bags and other items down the ramp to their vehicles.

Drivers always were in a hurry, and they always overloaded their carts so they would not have to make two trips in and out of the hub. A second trip was inefficient. If they had a really big load and one overloaded cart did not suffice, they packed two carts and tried to walk them down the ramp one behind the other. One overloaded cart was difficult to control. So were two full carts, more so if each of them were overloaded. If drivers went down the ramp too fast, they would dump their loads. Bottles and eggs were broken, and cans were dented. Stuff spilled and rolled everywhere. This caused a traffic jam. The drivers behind them couldn't use the ramp until it was cleared, and they would freak out. Desperate to get to their vehicles, they would attempt to carry their carts down the stairs or walk them down. Guess what ensued?

After I witnessed this circus, I manned the ramp and walked any drivers with overloaded carts to the bottom. When they arrived at the bottom of the ramp with loads intact, they were home free.

The ramp provided its own issue until yours truly came along. It was concrete, and there was a large seam at the bottom where the ramp and the sidewalk met. Sometimes when a cart hit that seam, the front wheels would catch, and the load would shoot off the front and hit the pavement. Different reason, same type of mess, and same result. Panic and followed by chaos. The drivers had to go back inside and get someone to re-pick the items. Time and inventory were lost. The customers did not receive their orders on time. The managers did not meet their quotas. Everyone lost except those guys waiting outside at the dumpsters.

Physical repairs to the ramp were required, but there was no way they would be performed. When I mentioned the problem to the big boss, he shrugged. It was obvious he did not care. The light bulb went on for me. Amazon did big things like converting warehouses and building new ones. It wasn't going to hire a cement contractor for a small repair job. Hmmm? What if the bottom of the ramp were covered, I wondered? I took a gaylord, cut it in half, folded it lengthwise, and used it to bridge the bottom of the ramp where it met the sidewalk. *Voila! La crevasse avait disparu.* The wheels of the carts didn't catch. The transition was smooth. There were no more messes. The drivers thanked me.

Now back to all of those cold storage bags I threw into gaylords. That process went on for a week, and I should have foreseen the future based upon the task. Sometimes it's not what they tell you to do or why; it's what is coming.

Chapter 13
Culled From the Heard

It's never a good thing when employees huddle together whispering. When the employees doing the whispering are management, it can be especially bad. The company is going under. A corporate takeover is in the works. Someone liked or well respected lost his or her job, or the entire workforce might be shown the door.

This was Amazon, the impersonal and relentlessly efficient beast. The hub at Cherry and Bliss was not closing its doors. Far from it. Amazon was acquiring new locations, turning them into hubs, and modernizing existing hubs. A major transformation had begun at the Cherry and Bliss hub. The rear of the building was being converted into an area at which packages would arrive by semi-trailer, moved to gaylords, removed, scanned, and loaded onto conveyor belts for deposit into cubicles and racks in the hub where they would be picked up by delivery van drivers. The fixtures in the rear third of the hub – shelves containing stock, dumpsters, freezers, and more – either had been relocated to the middle of the hub or eliminated from use. The front of the hub remained the same. For now.

I had not been scheduled to work for two days. All of that had begun in the two days that I was off.

Because it was priority one, the big boss was the point man on the rehab project. The number two man now was in charge of the rest of the hub: orders coming in, picking, and delivery every two hours. From him, it still went to the managers and from them to the associates. When orders were incorrect or didn't go out in time, the associates didn't feel the heat, however. Amazon tracked percentages. When the percentages weren't up to snuff, managers on duty for the underperforming shifts heard about it. When the numbers did not go up, and stay up, managers were fired.

The hub at Cherry and Bliss had issues that went beyond managers. A big one was the work force, which was comprised mostly of young people who did not have a work ethic. Some never previously held a job, while a few others did not feel like working or had not been able to hold a job for which they had to meet deadlines, quotas, or break a sweat. Many of my colleagues were college kids who did not want to get out of bed before noon. After they did finally get out of bed, they required a Starbuck's before a lengthy check of their phones or sinking into the abyss of video games. Working was way down on the list. Yet here they were in an Amazon hub.

A good thing was that so many of those who came in the door inexperienced and unmotivated departed with some work skills and an understanding of what was expected of a member of the workforce. There were a few who did not survive long enough to acquire the aforementioned.

When an associate was fired, it was because she or he could not follow the most simple of rules. They couldn't arrive on time after numerous chances and reminders to do so. They couldn't return from their breaks on time after numerous warnings to do so. They violated the rule prohibiting electronic devices in the work areas. They were escorted from the hub by security, or they gave up and quit. While I never re-connected with anyone fired, I hoped the departed used their firings as wakeups and went out and got real jobs. If they remained clueless, they had to move on to something lower paying but not necessarily easier such as fast food or ride sharing. Those who couldn't handle structure in any form might land just one step from rock bottom such selling "squares" on the Red Line.

Associates didn't have much, if anything, on the line, however. As the Dylan song lyric goes, "When you got nothin', you got nothin' to lose."

For managers, it was different. They were full-timers whose jobs featured benefits and stock options. There was upward mobility. As for what managers had to worry about besides Big Brother watching, the work world had changed such that there weren't as many grocery jobs or retail jobs for them to return to, which was why they were at Amazon in the first place. The world had gone online. It was why they were managers at Amazon.

Some of the managers were a little older. They had families to support. Or they were divorced and starting over. Whatever their personal situations, they were Americans with lifestyles and bills to pay. The pressure was on them to produce. No one wanted to miss a car payment, a mortgage payment, or have to go home and tell their spouse, "Honey, there won't be a check next week."

In my book, Amazon managers deserved much of the credit for the company's success. Every shift, they were handed a basket of challenges. Each manager was responsible either for part of the work force or part of the hub, and they might not have the same assignment each day. They worked where needed. So managers had to know what associates jobs were and how to perform properly. This was because a manager might have to quickly train a new hire, or she or he might have to perform an associate's tasks when a sufficient number of subordinates did not report to work. This happened every weekend, by the way. Managers also were required to know where products and equipment were located and how to use them. Being a manager was a guessing game that started the moment she or he walked in the door. They did not know what they would find. It was like jumping onto a moving vehicle.

Once on the moving vehicle, managers always had their eye on their laptop screen checking orders in progress, deliveries, inventory, and any one of a dozen other things. Because they tracked associates, they knew who was moving too slowly and would not pick their order and slam in time for delivery. Managers had to make sure that associates did finish on time, or it was their asses, not that of the associates. It was not uncommon to see a manager track down an associate in an aisle or at slam in an effort to improve a situation. There was no time for gossip between managers. The job did not include a time or a place for it.

Managers huddled together whispering made no sense. When I noticed it, I knew something was very wrong.

Not all of the managers participated in the unusual behavior – huddled together in two's or three's and whispering - and this also was telling. The non-participants kept their noses to the grindstone. They tended to their own business. They never looked up from their computer screens. These turned out to be the managers that stayed. In the span of a few weeks, those who had been huddling disappeared. No one from management explained the departures or introduced new managers that joined the hub. Old managers disappeared. Replacements appeared, and they were all business. The holdovers now rarely smiled or made small talk. Everyone in the hub knew what had happened, what was in progress. The Amazon higher ups, whoever was crunching numbers for the Cherry and Bliss hub, had not found the hub to be productive enough. Those determined not to be pulling their weight had been culled from the heard. The holdovers and the new people wanted to keep their jobs. As I was soon to learn, they would do whatever it took to keep them.

There was another addition to the poem. The tone no longer was light or upbeat.

> *Now Jeff Bezos, he pays us at Cherry and Bliss.*
> *Minimum wage*
> *Short break times.*
> *You can't take a piss.*
> *The managers are watching.*
> *There's not one thing they miss*
> *At the corner of Cherry and Bliss.*

Chapter 14
La Casa de Jimmy es Fabulosa

On the eve of the basketball tournament, I won a few more games than I lost and with it the opportunity to collect from Jimmy. If ever I required proof that winning comes with a cost, this would be it. Jimmy insisted I stop by his home to collect. The excuse he gave – his gout flared up – sounded legitimate. Yet I was suspicious. Jimmy wanted something, and if anyone could find a way to use gout to his advantage, it was Jimmy.

The alternative, which Jimmy offered, was to have Ed stop by my place with the money. While home delivery would have been much more convenient for me, I did not want Ed anywhere near my home. I cringed at the thought of my neighbors seeing him walk up the path to my door, and I certainly did not want him inside my dwelling. I told Jimmy I would stop by. He gave me his address and an appointed time for me to arrive. It was at that specified place and time that I got the shock of my life.

The house, which I was certain would be *La Guarida de La Iniquidad de Jaime,* actually was fabulous! Not certain I had the right address, I drove around the block. Twice.

I expected to find a large frame house teetering on the edge of physical collapse. There would be music blaring, a dozen or so cars, some double parked, in front and crammed into the driveway because of the perpetual dice game going on inside, empty beer cans and bottles strewn about like lawn ornaments, and a red neon sign flashing "JIMMY'S! YOUR SOUL AIN'T WORTH NUTIN'. SO I'LL TAKE YOUR DOUGH!"

I had expected The Devil's Roadhouse, but oh, contrere. Despite the dead of winter outside and the blackness of Jimmy's own soul, on that day I discovered the house to be, well . . . perfect. Its exterior was a beautiful red brick with tasteful light trim and green canvass awnings over the windows. The lawn and shrubs were immaculately manicured and there was a perfect white picket fence.

The American Dream? *Better Homes & Gardens*? Jimmy's abode? To borrow from Casey Stengel, whodda thunk it?

The inside front door was open wide, and I looked through the frosted glass window of a decorative storm dorm. More shock awaited inside. I saw a large living room with soft-colored walls and carpets, tasteful furniture, and expensive-looking items that were too tasteful to be mere bric-a-brac. And was that a work of art? At Jimmy's? Finally I refused to believe my eyes.

Above the fireplace in a gilded frame was a nude, a full-frontal portrait of a redheaded young woman posing in recline. On her face appeared a wry smile, which made me believe she was quite comfortable with her body. The artist must have loved her because every line and contour of her young body was perfect. The redheaded woman was familiar to me, and she was quite pleasing to look at.

Quite suddenly, there was contrast in the most base form. Ed appeared on the other side of the door, blocking my view. He was barefoot, gray in color, and alcoholic-militant-smoker skinny in baggy jeans and a faded AC/DC t-shirt. Ed sneered at me, pointed a boney yellow forefinger, and said, "Are you memorizin'? You'd better not be. Memorizin' is the kinda thing gets people inta trouble. Seeeer-ee-us truh-ble. An' hurt. Permanent." He stared me up and down as he reached out a hand to unlatch the storm door. After it clicked, he opened it slightly. "Get in here, boy. Jimmy's waitin'. An' don't be lookin' 'roun' so you can memorize anything while you're here. You get me?"

Ed already was walking away from me as I stepped inside of the house. "Latch that storm door and haul yer college-boy ass in here!" he shouted over his shoulder. I noticed a bulge at the left waistband under the t-shirt. If he did have a gun, I didn't want to be shot for something as ridiculous memorizin' - whatever that was - failing to latch a door, or because I had earned an advanced degree. I clicked it locked and followed Ed.

"Loser's here, Jimmy, and he was thinkin' 'bout memorizin' 'til I stopped 'im." Ed's version of my arrival was all about him saving the day. He jerked his left thumb back at me. "Jus' sayin'. Ya can't trust this 'un. Watch 'im." Ed glared at me from the corners of his eyes as he said it. He launched a departing sneer my way before turning and disappearing into the back of the house.

I shifted my stare from where Ed had been to Jimmy, whose immense frame was standing over the stove, and that quickly, we went from intensity back to surprises. So much for gout. If afflicted, Jimmy would not have been on his feet. Now what was that smell? Tomato sauce? Jimmy was cooking in his state-of-the-art kitchen which seemed to have hundreds of square feet of counter and cabinet space. There was a marble-topped island in the middle of the room, padded stools beneath it. A stove and refrigerator were built into the walls. Another marble-topped island with more stools were across the room, and atop that island were phones, pens, and legal pads. There also was an executive chair. It must have been where Jimmy worked when he was at home, which suddenly struck me as odd since I'd never imagined Jimmy anywhere except his bar.

Meeting atop one corner and mounted to form an angle were two large flat screen TVs, each with four—screen attachments. Pictures on but sound off, Jimmy had Jeopardy on a large screen while four different channels of news and sports flickered in the little boxes. Each screen could have been multiple choice answers. Jimmy might end up either a trivia question or a segment on the news.

The large man turned slightly and said, "Siddown, kid. Make yourself at home." Over his shoulder, he added. "You wanna a meatball sangwich? How 'bout a beer?" He nodded at a wine refrigerator built into one of the islands. "Go ahead. Get yourself one outta da lil' fridge. Grab me one, too."

Perfect as that kitchen seemed, I had a pretty good idea of where Jimmy's dirty fingers had been for the past forty-plus years and what they'd been doing. The never-ending stream of dirty money he had handled was enough to deter me. I declined the offer of the sandwich, opting instead for one of the bottles of beer Jimmy had chilling in his wine refrigerator. I removed two beers from it, took them to the table, and sat down in one of the stools at the closest island.

Looking at Jimmy as he prepared his sandwich, he seemed larger than when I'd last seen him. He turned profile, and I got a better look at the big man. Eyes framed by huge, bushy brows and high cheekbones encased in fat, jaw to shoulder seemed one great hanging jowl. The buttons of his pants and shirt were strained by his enormous belly, which began just below the sternum and ended just north of his knees. Jimmy's girth suggested a modern day Budhha, while his voice and mannerisms were Broderick Crawford in *Born Yesterday*. What a paradox. Or was it? To those whose religion was gambling, Jimmy was a deity. Yet the way he conducted himself hinted he might be performing.

As I pondered the possibilities, Jimmy and his huge sandwich, red sauce oozing from its bun, joined me at the island. He said, "Ya really oughtta have wunna dese, kid." He held it up for me to see before exacting a tremendous rip of bread and meat. Red sauce sauced dripped down his chin and onto his fingers from what was now half a sandwich. He shifted the sandwich from one hand to the other so he could lick his fingers clean. He addressed his chin after he'd finished the sandwich, which was only another few seconds.

Jimmy picked up the beer bottle I'd set in front of him and took several long gulps. He set the half-empty bottle down, looked at me happily, and let out a tremendous belch. This made him even more happy. He smiled, nodded to me, and said to me, "So?"

It was my turn, but I didn't know what I was supposed to say, and I was curious about to the art work. "That's an impressive a collection you have in the living room and hallways. You must have gone to a lot of trouble to find copies that appear so much like originals."

At that point, pensiveness replaced happiness. Jimmy's brows narrowed a little and a wry smile appeared on his face. I expected an explanation. Yet he said only, "Thanks." The look on his face indicated he would not to expand on his answer. He remain on subject but shifted slightly.

"Art is why I asked you here. I need someone ta do some research for me. You were a history teacher, weren't ya?"

I flinched. Were? Did Jimmy know I'd been forced out of my job and no longer worked as a teacher? He must have notice my reaction because he rephrased his questions.

"Your degree is history, right? And ya know how ta do historical research? Maybe ya know sumptin 'bout art."

"I do."

"Well, dat's good. I need somebody ta get me some, uh, detailed infamashun. I've made some major acquisitions, and I'm thinking about making a few more. Before I do anything foida . . . " (Here he hesitated to consider what he wanted to say.) ". . . ta help me determine what I already got and whether or not I should get any more of it, I need, uh, uh . . ." He thought for a few seconds before asking for help. "I think I'm looking for a v word."

"Verification?" I suggested.

"Boom. Dat's a good one. Do you think you could handle something like dat? Itza a payin' gig."

Jimmy stood up, walked over to a large vertical cabinet with a frosted glass window that said "Bread Box." He opened it, and removed a brown 8.5 by 11 envelope. He returned to the island with it, sat down, opened it, and removed a stack of one hundred dollar bills. His fast fingers counted out a number of the bills, and set them in front of me.

He told me, "Here's an advance."

I asked, "You keep your money in the bread box?"

"Yeah. Bread in da bread box." he said. "Funny? Right? Ha."

When I didn't react. Jimmy added, "Wha? Alluva sudden you ain't got no sensa humor?"

The part I thought was funny was that he thought it was funny. I smiled. Anxious to discuss the business at hand, I asked, "What do you need me to do?"

Jimmy launched into an explanation. "Look around. Da contractor who did this kitchen lost lotta money. Same widda landscaper. Hey, no problem fer me. Gambling doesn't care what someone does for a livin'. Why should I long as dey compensate me? Could be a preacher who owes me."

"Amen?" I interjected.

Jimmy growled what I suspected was a chuckle. He added, "Can't imagine what a preacher could do for me. Ain't takin' bibles ta settle debts. Hey, maybe a preacher could get me free pass inside da pearly gates." Amused by his own comment, Jimmy emitted what umistakably was a chuckle growl.

"Anyway, art collectors'r human. They just have better taste den most people. Dey gamble. Dey lose. Dey gotta pay. Makes 'em just like everybody else, an' dat's why I have some beautiful pieces. Wanna know what else makes 'em like everybody else? Ya can't trust 'em. So how do I know if got real McCoys?"

I was blown away. "What do you have?"

Jimmy said, "No, I'm tellin' ya dat's what you're gonna find out fer me. I wanna pay' ya for dat and yer uh . . ." He struggled to find the right word. I provided.

"Discretion."

"Ba-boom. Yer already earnin' yer money." He turned and yelled toward the back of the house, "Din' I tell ya? Dis guy's smart, Eddie?"

Ed shouted back, "Throw him out, Jimmy, before it's too late. Or better yet, lemme take 'im out to da forest preserve an' put a pill into 'im!"

I grimaced. "Complete discretion," I assured him before lowering my voice and asking, "I'll have to be here to make notes and take photos. Will Ed be a problem?"

His eyebrows narrowed. He did not understand. "How?"

"How can I get you the information you need if Ed suspects I have an ulterior motive?"

"Ulterior like on da outside a da house? I don' get it."

Finally there was real humor!

"Not quite," I explained. "After I arrived, he accused me of memorizing something. Does he think I might steal from you or make a phone call?"

From a back room, I heard Ed yell, "Don't trust 'im, Jimmy! Dat guy's bad news! Lemme pop 'im!"

Jimmy pursed his lips, frowned, and shook his head. "Ed ain't gonna bother ya', and yer not da type ta open yer mout'. Becuzzada ten thousand I'm payin' ya and fer udder reasons. Fer reasons you'll like."

The statement provided four essentials: assurance, confidence, financial incentive, and threat. He rose slowly from his seat and said, "Folla me."

I did as instructed. Jimmy led me down a hallway to a closed door. He removed a key from his right side pants pocket and unlocked the door. He opened the door and informed me, "My art collection. Check it out."

I stepped inside the room, which was spacious. It was filled with all types of works of art: paintings, small statuary, and jewelry. Some of the paintings were on the walls. More of them leaned against the walls. Some of the smaller items were on tables or pedestals. Others were scattered about the floor.

There was a painting was of a parlor scene with three young people, two of whom appeared to be playing musical instruments. Another painting was of small boats on a stormy sea. There were men in the boats, and one of them appeared to be Jesus. Another of the paintings was a colorful portrait of a young man. Based upon his attire and the background, it was set in the Middle Ages. Still another was a very beautiful piece, perhaps depicting life in the 1800s, of a man on his way somewhere.

Something in particular that caught my eyes was out of the way, situated in a corner on a decorative table. It was football-shaped but much smaller, and whatever it was sat upon a metal pedestal that interwoven like latticework. There appeared to be jewels or something encrusted in the little football or around it, but I could not be sure from that distance. Whatever it was, well, it was spectacular.

I was mesmerized. Jimmy brought me out of my trance. "Whaddaya think?"

I wasn't speechless, but the words did come slowly. I was still processing. "I think . . . I may have seen pictures of some of these in history books . . . Some of these . . . have been missing for years . . . decades . . . That egg-shaped piece . . . It can't possibly be . . ."

Jimmy informed me, "Dat's what yer gonna fine out."

I was surprised, flattered, and a little worried. "Why me?"

"C'mon," he told me. "Let's go back inta da kitchen 'n talk." I stepped out of the room. He locked it. He turned and led me back down the hallway. Jimmy sat down again and explained.

"What ya tol' me the udder day at da bar. Dat got ta me."

"About having a conscience?"

"Yeah, but not about me havin' one. About you. It's obveeus ya got one. Dat 'n ya don' need money. I think I can trus' ya."

From the back of the house, Ed yelled, "Don't trust 'im, Jimmy! He's like everybody else! He's gonna steal from ya! Now he knows too much. We gotta whack 'im and make his body disappear!"

Jimmy made a face as though he'd just eaten something sour. He shook his head and waves off Ed's words with his right hand. "Don' lisin ta dat. Ed gets carried away sometimes. He's over pertective."

Palms up, he looked at me and shrugged. "Waddaya tink. Ten grand jus' fer starters."

Well, in a way it would be a history job. All of those pieces, if authentic, had great stories tied to them. As Jimmy implied, to learn more about them, perhaps about where they'd been and how they got here, would be fascinating, the chance of a lifetime.

Jimmy and I did not have much in common, but we did share two things. We both liked money, and we were not employed full time, yours truly nowhere near to the advantage Jimmy had transformed his into. That sealed the deal. As I picked up the bills, I told him, "You can trust me to discreetly perform the task you require. I will do it as long as you understand the information provided may not be what you want to hear. When someone does your homework for you, there must be elements of acceptance and of trust."

"Somebody doin' my homework? Jimmy shrugged asked. "How d'ya think I got tru high school?"

Even more humor. Finally I did laugh.

Chapter 15
Es Wird Keine Poesie Geben!

The poem had disappeared from the bulletin board.

No sooner had I agreed to the well-paying gig for Jimmy than there were storm clouds on another employment horizon. My days as an Amazon employee were coming to a close. I could say the reason was a new manager named Amber, but that would not accurate. While I do suspect Amber had it in for me and made my job more difficult, I could have bent to the rules and stayed. Amazon was a transition job. It was time to go. Amber simply relayed the message.

Amber was one of managers transferred to the Cherry and Bliss hub after most members of the previous group went out the door. She was not personable or flexible. She was rigidly efficient. Everything Amber did - a task, a communication, whatever - she did it without a trace of emotion. When an associate approached Amber with a question or to talk about something, they might get an answer. If they did, the response would be terse and without facial expression or eye contact because Amber refused to look at associates. I recall co-workers asking her for clarification on an assignment and receiving not so much as the twitch of an eyebrow, only stone silence in return. It was a tactic. If you don't make eye contact with whoever you speak with, the encounter is impersonal. When you refuse to respond, the intent is to intimidate. Many associates grumbled about Amber. No one liked her, but at first, no one wanted to challenge her.

Amber was the perfect person to resolve an issue that, to the displeasure of Amazon, had been embraced by the old managers. It pertained to hours worked by associates. The managers who were fired had looked the other way when it came to associates working forty or more hours per week. At that time, Amazon did not allow associates to work forty hours. Associates got away with it because managers encouraged it. A manager would tell an employee he or she knew to be a good worker, "Can you show up for my shift tomorrow? Don't worry about your hours."

This was to the advantage of the manager. When she or he was short of manpower during a shift, the managers had to pick, stock shelves, and do whatever it took to get through the day without deliveries being botched or late. It had gotten to the point that yours truly and a few other industrious associates took extra hours for granted. We would show up and clock in because unmotivated members of the workforce would not show up for their shifts. We'd arrive for the shift before ours, for which we weren't scheduled, and work through. We would clock from eight to twelve hours.

A few hungry associates such as yours truly were working over forty hour per week, and it went on for quite awhile. We compared notes on the QT.

"How many hours did you get last week?" a co-worker named Babe would ask.

"Almost fifty," I replied because most weeks I did.

"Good for you! I got forty four, but I'll catch up to you next week."

Babe was a large woman, over six-feet tall and maybe two hundred pounds, but her looks belied her personality. She was a twenty-five years old single mom, and she was a sweetheart. More important for Amazon's purposes, she had a great work ethic, and she was so smart and personable that she trained new hires. All of the associates loved Babe because she was so helpful. So did the managers, and she seemed to love everyone and her job. Until Amber came along.

As for all of those extra hours, it was a profitable conspiracy while it lasted, and who did it hurt? Certainly not Amazon. The extra money we earned did not prevent Bezos from buying another major newspaper, a professional sports franchise, or from taking Lauren Sanchez around the world on his yacht. We were good employees who knew what we were doing, and we weren't looking to become full-time employees for benefits. All we wanted was a bigger check, and we always gave a good hour of work for a good hour of pay.

In those days, none of that mattered to Amazon corporate. Associates were not supposed to get forty hours. Period. Managers at the Cherry and Bliss hub received another order from high. *Associates shall work less than forty hours or else!* The arrival of Amber and other new managers signaled change. Suddenly they were in our ears if not our faces. One day at the end of a four-hour shift that I'd booked, I was walking through the hub fully intending to continue another four hours. I heard an authoritarian voice from behind me. It was Amber.

"Your shift is over. Clock out. Now."

I turned and looked at her, but I didn't say a word. I simply changed directions and walked to the break room where the login clock was located. By the time I walked out of the hub, Amber already was at the manager's station near the door. Her eyes were riveted to the screen of her laptop, though I suspected she watched me through their corners. And I would swear that for the first time, tiny creases formed the start of a smile at the corners of her lips. I didn't wait to see the finished product and continued walking. That happened a few times with Amber. The confrontation and the near smile of her mission accomplished. She always found me at the end of my shift to remind me to clock out.

The last straw for me was when she informed me my job was to pick. I tried to tell her that I was more valuable to her in other areas, but she didn't want to hear it. With neither emotion nor eye contact, she said, "When I need you to do anything else, I will let you know."

I walked out of the hub that day, and I did not return. Amazon had been a good gig while it lasted. My time there renewed my spirit and helped me regain my confidence. By coincidence, after work I was supposed to meet with Jimmy. He had left me a message to meet him at his home that evening so we could talk more about what he needed me to do. That message was the most exciting thing about the day, but that was quickly to change. Sitting in my car in the parking lot across the street from the hub, I was going to turn the ignition when a police car, emergency lights flashing and siren blaring, sped up the hub entrance. Two police officers went inside. Maybe two minutes later, an ambulance pulled up. Two paramedics went inside carrying a stretcher.

I hadn't heard gunshots. There must have been an accident. I waited. Eventually Amber was wheeled out strapped onto the stretcher. Babe, in handcuffs and flanked by the officers, emerged and was placed in the back of the squad car.

An associate who clocked out just after I did witnessed what happened and described it. As she had with me, Amber approached Babe and told her to clock out. Babe wanted an explanation, but Amber refused to acknowledge her, spun around, and attempted to walk away. Babe grabbed Amber by the shoulder, spun her back around, and decked her. The associate told me that Amber was out cold before she hit the floor. It was one more reason for everyone to like Babe.

Jimmy could wait. I discreetly followed the police car to the station house. Once I had the location, I drove to an ATM and withdrew cash. I drove back to the police station, parked, went inside, and talked the desk sergeant into allowing me to see Babe.

"My girlfriend texted me that she was being arrested. I think they brought her here," I explained to him. I realized too late that I didn't know Babe's real name. Before he could ask for it, I quickly described her.

He gave me a funny look before telling me. "Go around the corner and enter the first conference room on the right. I'll have her brought in."

Approximately 15 minutes later, the door opened, and Babe walked in. At first, she was surprised to see me. I stood up, and we hugged. I pulled back and told her. "Thanks for doing what we all wanted to do."

Babe was dead serious when she said, "She disrespected me. I don't take that from anybody. She added, "I boxed as a professional for a few years."

"Nice," I said with admiration before cautioning her, "Don't mention that at the arraignment."

We sat down. I took out my wallet, removed the five hundred dollars I'd withdrawn at the ATM, and slid it across the table at Babe. She looked at it and asked, "What's this?"

"You're going to need bail money. You can't stay in a jail cell all night."

Babe looked at the money, thought for a few seconds, and nodded before picking up the money and putting it in her shirt pocket. It was the smart thing. Our hands were on the table, and she reached across and put her right hand on mind. "Thanks," she said sincerely. "How will I pay you back?"

"You already did."

"You know, I always liked you." She hesitated before resuming, "I always thought we might . . ."

Before she could finish, a police officer open the door and announced, "Time's up." He looked directly at Babe, pointed a finger at her, and signaled toward the doorway. "You. Let's go. We got approval from the ASA. You're headed to 26th and California."

26th and Cal. Ugh. I once heard a criminal defense attorney describe it as "a cesspool." I hoped I had given her enough money to bond or buy her way out.

Babe read my mind. She stood up and assured me, "I got this." She stood up and strode out of the room. It was the last time I ever would see her.

I had no second thoughts about giving Babe the five hundred dollars. Growing up, my parents always told us, "Whatever good works you do for people will come back to you one thousand fold."

I always believed what they told me. I just didn't know how absolutely true it was.

Chapter 16
Who Croaked Jimmy?

It was just after 8 p.m. when I parked my car across from Jimmy's home, I was two hours late. We'd agreed to meet at six, but my business with Babe had to be more important than whatever was going on at Jimmy's, and I guessed the big man would understand, that he would enjoy hearing the story of how my co-worker had knocked out the boss. He probably would be so amused when he learn each was a woman that he would chuckle growl.

Lights shown from the back of Jimmy's home, but not the front. I followed the sidewalk to the front door, rang the doorbell once, and waited. Because there was no answer, I pressed it a second time. Ed probably was tending bar, and Jimmy was a slow mover. Still something didn't seem right. After I waited a sufficient time, I tried the door. It was unlocked. I opened it and stepped inside.

"Hello. Anybody home? Jimmy?"

Oh, man. What had I done? What if Jimmy were not home and Ed stepped out of the darkness. "Appointment, my ass!" I imagined Ed shouting before he shot me for trespassing, breaking and entering or whatever else he could imagine. I quickly opened the door and stepped back outside.

Neither Jimmy nor Ed appeared, however, and that renewed my suspicions and my courage. I stepped back inside. "La Belle Petite Rousse," as I had begun to think of her, stared at me from the darkness. Her smile boarded on a smirk, and she looked so familiar. Perhaps she was something Jimmy had acquired and liked so much that instead of locking her away in a room, he hung her above the mantle where he could enjoy her beauty.

Slowly I walked the hallway toward the kitchen. Maybe whoever was at home was in the bathroom or the basement? You never would know it by Ed, but he must have done laundry some time. Perhaps Jimmy was in the backyard or garage? Someone had to be somewhere. Possibilities passed through my mind, but they weren't good. Jimmy never would leave the house unlocked.

Had there been a gambling raid? If so, the cops would have permitted Jimmy to lock his home, but who was I talking about? Jimmy paid off. There would be no way the local cops burst, and had a higher-up agency had been after Jimmy, the locals would have tipped him someone was coming. That service always was included in a payoff. Maybe that was it, I thought. Jimmy fled after receiving a call. The next sign loaned itself to that possibility. Standing at the entrance of the kitchen, I not only smelled the tomato sauce and meatballs, I heard it. The concoction bubbled loudly as if it wanted to jump out of the pot, a sure sign that Jimmy had been there recently. The combination was percolating, and I needed to turn it off before it overflowed or burned. I stepped around a marble island toward the stove.

On the floor lying face down between the marble island and the stove was Jimmy. A small river of red had run from his skull down the back of his neck and onto the floor, and it wasn't tomato sauce. I winced. While I had zero interest in touching Jimmy, it was a special occasion. I reached down to check for a pulse. Nothing was cooking. Jimmy seemed as dead as last week's meatball sandwich. Never having been confronted by a situation like this at any time in my life made it challenging. Yet I knew instinctively what to do. I walked around Jimmy's body and turned off the meatballs and sauce. It was what Jimmy would have wanted.

Somebody apparently had punched his ticket in his own house, in his beloved kitchen, and judging by the Italian bread roll on the plate next to the stove and the sweating full bottle of Michelob alongside of it, just before dinner. I took a closer look around the room for evidence of what happened. There was no sign of a struggle. No furniture was overturned. Nothing was broken or scattered except Jimmy's cranium.

Atop the counter where Jimmy lay was a large cast iron skillet. It was the only cookware on the countertop, and it was out of place. I bent toward it to take a closer look without touching it. A small bloody clump of hair stuck to a portion of the rim, and blood was smeared on the side of it. The skillet was the murder weapon. Jimmy must have sustained several good whacks with it.

It did not take a forensic scientist to piece together what had happened. Within the last hour, Jimmy had a guest. At some point during the visit, Jimmy turned his back to fix himself a meatball sandwich. When he'd done so, the visitor had flattened Jimmy's skull. As for who could it have been, the crime scene was a clue. Jimmy mentioned that he settled all accounts at the bar. Customers did not come to his home. The killer must have been someone Jimmy dealt with on a personal basis.

When there wasn't a spouse, the roommate always was the prime suspect. Could Ed and Jimmy have had a falling out? Method said no. The murder weapon was a skillet, not a gun. Were Ed going to kill Jimmy, he'd have pulled his piece and shot him. Intellect was another factor that eliminated Ed. He probably couldn't organize his sock drawer let alone carry out a crime that included escape or resulted in exoneration. Not that he could think that far ahead either. Scratch that one, I decided. No, the best reason to eliminate Ed as a suspect was that he would not kill the Golden Goose. He couldn't if he ever again desired to eat and sleep in a place of quality instead of a jail cell.

After all of this flashed through my mind, I took a moment to consider the possibilities as I stared down at Jimmy. I was curious, and I had a hunch that I did not identify until later. The hunch led to an impulse, and the impulse was a game changer. Had Jimmy also been robbed?

I walked down the back hallway to the room where Jimmy kept the artwork. The door was closed, so I tried the handle. The room was locked. The art must have been inside. What were the odds the killer would rob Jimmy of the art and simply close the door when they exited. The odds were zero.

If the art had not been touched, had the killer been after money? I walked back into the kitchen, to the bread box, and opened it. This time tere weren't envelopes inside. There were packs of $100 bills bundled and banded, and they were stacked one atop the other, filling the bread box bottom to top. Whoever had ended Jimmy's life either hadn't been looking for money or hadn't known where to look. The latter was one more reason to eliminate Ed as a suspect because as Jimmy's assistant, confidant, and in capacities I preferred not to imagine, Ed certainly knew where money was stashed.

This is where impulse took over. The amount of money inside the bread box was substantial. It would have been enough to keep the late Jimmy in meatballs for a long time. It appeared to be enough to take care of someone for the rest of their life.

Somebody was going to get it, and it might as well may be me.

I picked up a dish towel, walked back to where the art stash was kept, and wiped clean the doorknob. I returned to the kitchen and wiped my finger prints from the stove where I had turned off the burner. Dish towel still in hand, I opened drawers and cabinets until I found three large shopping bags. Quickly and carefully I stacked the packs of money inside of the shopping bags, giving each of the bags a test lift to ensure it would handle the weight. Each was up to the task.

I wiped my prints from the bread box. I carried the towel with me to the front door, where I wiped the handle I turned to get in. I paused, looked back at the redhead. She smirked at me. Did that mean she approved of my taking the money? After using the dishtowel to open the storm door, I wiped it clean before placing the dish towel into one of the bags. Before exiting, I made the sign of the cross, sighed, and said aloud, "God bless you, Jimmy. Rest in peace, and thank you."

I was rich.

Chapter 17
Existentialism Kicks In

I was terrified.

What the hell had I just done? Ten minutes tops inside of Jimmy's, and I had made a lifetime mistake, perhaps a life ending one.

Immediately after fleeing Jimmy's, I drove home, ran inside the house with the bags of money, and set them atop the dining room table. I ran back to lock the door, and pulled every shade and blind before turning on a light. I took a deep breath. I was about the count the money and learn just how much I'd made off with.

At that point, my emotion quickly went from excitement to terror.

What the hell had I done? Not done? I had been at a crime scene, but I had neglected to report the crime. I had stolen money, and that money I either had been stolen or it had been generated from a criminal enterprise. The money was hotter than a bubbling pot of meatballs and sauce. The local cops, the FBI, the IRS, Ed, and crooks Jimmy had been in cahoots with all might come looking for me.

Just as suddenly terror dissipated. Remorse and shame replaced it, and a revelation ensued.

I was not me anymore!

Who the hell was I? What had I become?

What a tough dose of existentialism. It was as though Sartre, Kierkegaard, de Beauvoir, and Campus all kicked me in the balls.

"No!" I cried out. "No! No! No!"

That was followed by, "Dumb, dumb, dumb!" and a whack in forehead with the palm of my right hand.

I was not raised to be dishonest. I was not a crook, though I wouldn't make such a ridiculous claim. Thank you, Richard Nixon. I'm certain I had stolen something small somewhere along the line, but that didn't mean I was a crook of any magnitude, and I wasn't about to continue down that path.

I was going to reverse it.

Calmly this time and absolutely determined, I picked up the shopping bags full of bundles of $100 bills and walked out of the back door of my house. I set down the bags and locked the back door. I picked up the bags, brought them to my car, set them on the back seat, got into the car, and started it.

That last verse of "Hotel California" was not coming true for yours truly. The money was not mine. I was returning it to Jimmy's.

Chapter 18
The Orange Car and Karma

There was a car in the driveway.

Because it was so dark outside, I couldn't tell if it was a sports car or a compact. The distinct thing about the small car was its color. It was orange.

I drove past twice. After the first time, I went around the corner and parked. I waited five minutes and drove around again. Slowly. In the dim light and shadows, it was impossible to read the license number. Other than the orange color, the only other discernable detail about the car was a minor one. The rear passenger side tire was missing its hubcap.

Whose car was it? I had no idea, but I had to guess it was Ed's. Who else would be at Jimmy's at that hour? And there were more lights on inside the house, which also pointed to Jimmy's flunky. There was no way I could stop and snoop around Jimmy's to find out. If anyone saw me outside of the car, if anyone so much as noticed my car slow down in front of Jimmy's, they might describe me or my car or give my plate number to the police. You know how people are when it comes to murders. They want to get involved. They may not have accurate information or know the victim or his family, but they're going to get their two cents in. The police would search everywhere for a car matching the description of mine and run a check on any vehicle with so much as a partial plate number.

Eventually yours truly would be brought in for questioning.

What if a someone who saw me wasn't civic-minded? What if they were unsavory? Cops would be bad. Associates of Jimmy would be worse. Much worse.

I wasn't they type to kick myself, but when I did, I was good at it. Right through the goalposts every time.

I should have dialed 9-1-1 when I found Jimmy dead on the kitchen floor, and I should not have taken his money. That I had not done one and had done the other brought bad karma.

Now I could not return the money.

Crap. What was I going to do?

Chapter 19
Getting My Halo

Get out of town was the answer.

After driving away from Jimmy's the second time, I hadn't paid attention to where I was going. By the time I regained cognizance, my car was speeding north on I-57 toward downtown Chicago, and I let it follow that course until just past the White Sox ballpark when I steered my vehicle to the I-55 junction and drove west. Bingo! About twenty miles and thirty minutes later, just off of I-55 and east of County Line Road approaching Burr Ridge, I noticed a sign advertising a Holiday Inn Express. I remembered hearing it offered extended stay rates. I spotted the hotel, passed it, exited I-55 at Route 83, made a left, and re-entered I-55. I exited at County Line Road, turned onto a curved frontage road, and pulled into the hotel parking lot.

That Holiday Inn Express appeared to be perfect. Then again, so had Jimmy's house, which at that moment must have featured a dead fat guy on the kitchen floor and people standing over him wondering how he got there. I parked, looked around, and, satisfied that no one was around, locked the shopping bags inside the trunk.

The hotel lobby was small and drab. A young woman was at the desk. I figured her to be a married mom with kids. Why else would she be there? It wasn't the glamour, the money, or the shift that went with being a night clerk.

"I'm in town on business and need to book an extended stay. May I pay in cash?"

The woman smiled politely when she informed me, "You can pay with cash, but we require a credit card on file for security purposes."

"That is a problem. You see, my wallet was stolen.

"I'm sorry, sir. It's corporate policy. You can't book a room without a credit card or ID."

"I see. Well, thank you," I replied before pivoting and walking out of the lobby and to the trunk of my car. I unlocked the trunk and removed a stack of bills. I peeled ten bills from the stack and tossed the stack back inside a bag."

The lobby still was empty when I returned, which made it convenient for me to transact business. I guessed how much it would take, and I slid three one hundred dollar bills across the counter at the night clerk. I was prepared to go to ten bills if she played hard ball. The woman looked at the bills, back at me, and asked sweetly and sincerely, "Now that's not nearly enough for me to trust you and put my job on the line, is it?"

I asked, "How much would be enough?"

She didn't have to think long before rattling off, "Four kids, an ex-husband who can't afford child support, a boyfriend working a near-minimum wage job, two past due credit card bills, and the landlord coming for the rent day after tomorrow."

That was all I needed to hear. As I turned and walked out a second time, there was regret and desperation in her voice as she called out to me, "Hey, mister, wait. I didn't mean to squeeze you. Three hundred is good. Let's talk."

I waved my hand without looking back. It was too late.

When I returned a few minutes later, she looked puzzled and a little afraid. The thought might have crossed her mind that I was sent by the corporate office, and she was about to be fired. When I put two stacks of hundreds on the counter, she beamed. The bills disappeared from the counter so fast that it was as though they'd vaporized.

"You don't have to fill out a card. I have all your information, including your name."

"You do? What's my name?"

"It's Angel," she said, and she handed me a key. She added, "If you need to watch the parking lot or make a quick getaway, this is the best room."

The hotel was as isolated and inconspicuous as could be in an urban area. It was around the bend of a two-way access road that mostly ran parallel to I-55 north, yet was inaccessible directly from the interstate. A driver had to exit, travel south to the next intersection, and make a u-turn and drive several blocks to get to it. The parking lot horseshoed around the hotel from one side of the front entrance and around the back to the other side of the front entrance. As for my room, the desk clerk was right. It was a third floor corner next to the back stairs, and I could watch my car from the window. I also could watch the access road. Inside, the unit was a studio with a bathroom and small kitchen. It featured a stove, microwave, refrigerator, and cable TV. There was once-weekly housekeeping service. Sheets, pillowcases, towels, toiletries were available twenty-four-seven if I stopped by the front desk.

Before I went up to my room that first time, I asked the woman who'd checked me in to tell me the days and hours she worked. I thought it best that whatever I wanted, I deal with her. Also before I locked myself in that first night, I went grocery and clothes shopping. There was a grocery store and a Target on Route 83, which was the next exit on I-55. I needed food and I needed clothing. When I returned, I made two trips and brought everything up to the room via the back way. I showered. Before I went to sleep, I wedged a chair in front of the door.

Weeks went by. At first, I did not sleep well, and I dared not leave the hotel unless it was absolutely necessary.

Chapter 20
Fancy Meeting You Here

Sleeping became easier. Absolutely necessary became more frequent as boredom set in. Staring out of the window and not seeing sinister characters or creeps like Ed both comforted and emboldened me. Trips to grocery stores and restaurants became more frequent. Part of my daily routine became driving a mile and a half to the Dunkin Donuts restaurant on Route 83. I liked the coffee - it was much more preferable than the complimentary coffee available in the lobby - plus I wanted to get away from the hotel and see people. Not to interact with anyone, but to see people and walk among them.

The Dunkin Donuts seemed safe. The location was at the south corner of a strip mall next to a physical therapy office that always was closed when I arrived. A muffler shop was the business to the rear. A car dealer was across the street. The Dunkin Donuts took up a double storefront, and there was a large seating area inside. There were tables and chairs outside. Old guys who nursed their coffees over reminiscences and grumblings sat outside when the weather was good.

One beautiful morning when I arrived, the geezers were outside, and I nodded hello at them as I approached. They nodded back without interrupting their gabbing. Priorities. Mine was coffee. The inside of the restaurant was moderately crowded. A few customers sat at tables. There were half a dozen customers ahead of me in line. I stood there for maybe thirty seconds before someone behind me whispered, "Still doing the *Times* Crossword?"

It wasn't a voice I'd not heard recently. Yet I recognized it. Suzie Chen? From B.O. High? I turned around.

"I miss that," she added. "How have you been? You just kind of . . . "

I finished the thought for her. "Disappeared."

Suzi nodded as though she understood. "You know, they tricked you into quitting. You didn't have to give up your teaching job."

"What? Where did you hear that?"

"A school board member had it in for you. She told the assistant principal to find a way to get rid of you. He has eyes on the superintendent job. So he agreed to be her hatchet man."

She smiled sympathetically. "In other words, you got conned. You got and you were screwed."

The story was more shocking than the verbs. Yet it was plausible. School politics were no different than politics anywhere, and over the years I'd heard stories from other staff members.

Suzie pointed ahead. The line in front of me had disappeared. It was my turn to order. "Get me a black coffee with two sugars. We'll sit and chit chat."

A few minutes later, I set down two cups of coffee at a table in the far corner of the restaurant. Suzie was ready for hers. She removed the lid of hers and took a sip before I pulled out my chair and sat down. Before getting back to the subject of my resignation, I had to get the most important question out of the way. "What are you doing here?"

"It's spring break. I live in Willowbrook just a few blocks from here. I sometimes stop here on my way to school. I'm out this early because I have some appointments."

Route 83 was a dividing line between Burr Ridge and Willowbrook, and the area was a convenient drive to B.O. High. That part made sense. I ignored the question about where I lived.

"How do you know about the board member and the principal?"

"There was gossip at school about how and why you left, but none of the rumors made sense. Not that we know each other well, but based upon what I observed, you're not the irresponsible type. Certainly not the type to be fired. Eventually I was able to learn from a reliable source that you were forced to resign and why.

"Who is the board member?" After she gave me the name, I told her, "I don't know her. I've never met her."

Suzi shook her head that I was wrong. "Her daughter was one of your students last year. There was an issue with a project."

That made it easy. "Okay, I remember a student with that last name and what happened, but it wasn't anything unusual. She procrastinated, so her project wasn't ready on the due date. I granted her an extension. She finally submitted, but her project was incomplete. She hadn't followed the guidelines. We discussed that, and I gave her one more shot."

Suzie nodded. "I'll bet that one wasn't up to snuff."

"The end result was a sub-standard project submitted very late for which she did not receive a failing grade, just a low one."

"Which caused her semester grade to be low. Which caused her GPA to drop. That was the issue."

"A board member went after me for that?"

"In Texas, cheermoms put out hits on their daughter's rivals."

"If I worked in Texas . . . I still probably wouldn't have seen that coming."

Suzi changed the subject.

"How long had you been teaching? I mean, maybe you just became too comfortable." She segued again. "Anyway, it's fortunate I happened to run into you here today. I didn't know how to get in touch with you. All of a sudden you were gone. No one from school has been able to get in touch with you. "

Suzi was good at speaking. I was good at listening, which I did. Hard. No one was able to get in touch with me since I ran out of Jimmy's with two bags full of hundred dollar bills? That wasn't what she said, but she didn't have to. More would be coming. Much more. It did, smoothly and to the point.

Suzie said, "I can help you get your job back."

What a good hook! I was impressed. Yet it didn't yet have bait that might cause me to bite. Suzi gauged my reaction and understood this. I studied. Suzi calculated. She was confident. Completely undeterred. It was a different Suzi than the one I thought I knew, and I was tempted to ask her success rate. That Suzi must have closed a lot of sales calls. She actually believed I would buy what she was selling, that it simply would take her a little longer.

I was back to extrapolating about Suzi. According to my new calculations, he would throw in some twists and a plea.

"The guy hired to replace you lasted only three weeks. One day during his prep, he walked out to his car, drove away, and didn't come back. There have been substitute teachers in your classes ever since. The students aren't learning."

She waited. She sighed emphatically.

"Your students need you. The school needs you.

"And I miss our doing the Crossword together."

Okay, more than one plea. "We didn't actually do it together," I pointed out.

There was confusion and exasperation in her voice when she said, "You do want your job back." It wasn't a question.

I had not thought about getting my job back, and I was skeptical that a rookie teacher with whom I was barely acquainted could help me do so. Okay, it was Suzi Chen, the woman who I once thought I would like to spend the rest of my life with. Forced to live in the real world, I'd become concerned about having a rest of my life, plus at that moment I was worried about the time and other people factors.

Someone was on the way. How long before they, like Suzi, just happened to walk into the Dunkin Donuts and asked me a question? Or maybe they wouldn't ask. They would demand. With all of the powers of their persuasion. Powers that exceeded Suzi's. I looked around before I asked, "And you can make that happen?"

"I can put the right words in the right ears. With that and with the help of the union, you could be back at school by the first of next month. That's only two weeks away."

Suzie was very convincing. What a terrific saleswoman. She could sell anything. Almost. I had been drinking coffee while I listened, but I was finished. The coffee had been enjoyable, as had been the performance. Now it was time to go. I asked the question.

"In return for your help, what will I be required to do?"

"Give me the money you took from Jimmy's."

Just like that, my requirement was out in the open, inevitably and finally, and Suzi had explained it so pleasantly, as though I would believe it was not only the right thing to do. It was the prudent thing. Safe and without consequences.

I was standing but not looking at Suzi. I was watching out the window when I asked, "Do you drive an orange car?

"Orange? No, I hate that color."

I turned to look at her. "Where is your car?"

"It's right there." She pointed out the window at the front of the store. "The robin's egg blue Beemer convertible." Based on the plate, I decided she was telling me the truth. It was a California vanity plate. "Su Zee 1.

"Why?"

I was about to answer when the orange car drove past. I knew it was the same one because the passenger side rear hubcap was missing. I could not determine who was driving the car. It didn't matter.

Chapter 21
The Musty Smell of Discovery

Suzi did not have time to react. That was how fast I was out the door, in my car, and down the road. I glanced in my rearview mirror and saw her exit the restaurant, stare in my direction, and turn to look in the direction the orange car had gone. As for everything she had told me, if true, it was enlightening but far less important than what I surmised.

Suzi was connected to Jimmy, and the nature of the connection pertained to business and money. Suzi had been looking for me, and she had finally found me. I hoped Suzie had not been tailing me, that she did just happen to enter the Dunkin Donuts and step into line behind me. I had no way of knowing, but I hoped. It might have made things simpler for me. Fortunately, I'd already planned for complications, for worst-case scenarios. All of that and more was what I thought about as I sped down Route 83 and onto Interstate 55 east toward the city.

The car wasn't the only thing speeding. My brain was in high gear, and I reviewed what I needed to do. There was no way I could return to the hotel. Ever. Suzie and whoever she may have been working with knew I lived there. I guessed they wanted to try subtlety first, all of those details from the beautiful Suzi and the get-your-job-back assurance. I did appreciate the break Suzi and whoever was in the orange car afforded me: attempting to sneak up on me for the money. There would be no such niceties from here on. If I returned to the hotel, I would be a sitting duck for their Plan B, whatever that was. Much later I could phone the hotel desk to inform the woman there that I had unexpectedly been transferred to a new jobsite and to ask her to pack and store what I had left behind. I would promise to send payment, which I would, in cash.

My second most important thought post-coffee with Suzie Chen was a repeat of when I had fled Jimmy's: make myself impossible to find, and just as the Chicago skyline came into full view, an idea popped into my head. I changed lanes and steered the car from east to an off ramp south. I was on the way back to the South Side. There were a few things I needed to see and do. Maybe they would not suspect I'd return so soon.

Yep. I was going home. I would be there briefly. I was comforted that I did not see the orange car in my rearview mirror as I sped south.

The first two items on the agenda were drive-bys. I wanted to see Jimmy's bar and his home. I had no knowledge of what had transpired at either since Jimmy was murdered, and I wanted to see if it was business as usual or if it had shut down. One pass of each told me everything.

There was nothing unusual at the earthly home of the not-so-dearly departed. A small late-model pickup truck sat in Jimmy's driveway. If it belonged to Ed, there was a complication. That meant Ed didn't own the orange car. Because I needed who was following me, I hoped the pick up did not belong to Ed.

Worse case: Ed owned the truck. If so, maybe Jimmy's family was allowing him to live there until the estate could be finalized. If Jimmy had a family, and if he had a will. The only relative of Jimmy that I knew of was his uncle, and that was another thing, two other things actually.

The story of Jimmy's murder appeared in local newspapers three weeks afterward, which was odd. Why did it take so long for a murder in a nice neighborhood to make the news? According to the story, Jimmy's accordion-playing uncle was the perpetrator. He killed Jimmy after an argument over money. That part of the story made perfect sense.

The uncle had fallen for a con known as the Canadian Lottery Telephone Scam. He'd received a call from a sweet-talking woman who informed him that he had won a fortune in the Canadian Lottery. All he had to do to receive his winnings was pay the taxes. The woman said she was an agent of the Canadian Lottery System. If the uncle wired the tax money, she would wire his winnings.

The uncle wired the money. Nothing came from north of the border except for another call explaining there was another charge. The uncle was told to wire more money. He did so. All he received was another call.

That the uncle did not smell a rat and inform authorities were his undoing. He continued to wire money. In for a penny, he was in for a pound. Transitioning from Charles Dickens to Mark Twain, the latter said, "If sense were common, everyone would have it."

When the uncle's pennies and pounds ran out, he took out a second mortgage on his home. Still no lottery winnings. He borrowed from family and friends, the exception being his nephew, the relative who had the most money. Jimmy's contribution? He bluntly told the uncle that he was being conned, which upset the uncle but did not deter him. There is another great quote, by someone infamous, not famous, and which I do not believe ever appeared in a mainstream news story until this one. Jimmy told his uncle, "Get yer head outta yer ass!"

Funny and it got the point across. Okay, too well for Jimmy's purposes.

Eventually the uncle was broke and out of borrowing options. Yet he remained certain he could get the Canadian Lottery money from the conwoman. Again he went to see Jimmy at his home, and this time he offered to split the award with him. "What'r gonna split wid me? Dere ain't no money!" They argued in his nephew's kitchen. Jimmy concluded by informing his uncle that he was a fool and that he should go to hell. Incensed, the uncle picked up a skilled and struck Jimmy in the back of the head. He stormed out of the house and left Jimmy lying on the floor to die.

The next day, the cops arrested the uncle after receiving an anonymous tip, at which time he confessed.

If the story of how Jimmy died was odd, even more unusual was what followed. Or rather what did not. A death notice for Jimmy did not appear in any newspapers. Nor did any mortuaries list his death notice. Whatever happened to Jimmy post mortem was private, so private that no one knew the arrangements. Had that newspaper story not appeared three weeks after his death, most people wouldn't have known Jimmy died and how it happened.

I thought about all of that as I drove past the bar, which was open. There were cars in the parking lot and on the street in front. Whoever was calling the shots regarding Jimmy's estate embraced his philosophy of business as usual.

Last and most risky, which meant I had to be very quick, I stopped at my home. My reasoning was that Suzi and whoever she worked with would not figure I would go there immediately after our conversation at the Dunkin Donuts. Logically, Suzi and company would determine my next move was to leave the state since remaining in the area had not worked for me. It would make sense for them to have eyes at Midway and O'Hare airports.

I parked the car and hurried into the house after looking around to make sure no one was watching or following. It was cold inside. I thought I'd left the heat on. Did the furnace go out? I checked the thermostat. It was off. I could have sworn I turned the furnace down but not off when I left. How could I have made such a stupid mistake? When I turned on the furnace, it didn't kick in, however. There were no sounds of the furnace activating or of the rush of air into the vents. Yet there was a musty smell.

The furnace was in the basement. I descended only three stairs before I stopped. Water spewed from a broken pipe above. My basement was under water. Items not anchored or heavy enough to withstand the water swirled aimlessly. There had been a cold spell three weeks ago. When the furnace went out, a pipe must have burst. I cursed myself. Three weeks of non-stop water was plenty long enough to do damage to a home. Now the water had to be shut off, the basement pumped out, and the pipe and furnace repaired. The standing water accounted for the odor.

Back upstairs, I was just about to pick up the phone to call a plumber, but I stopped. No! I had set the furnace before I left. Someone had been here since and turned it off. The water damage was a message. Or maybe it was a way to find me. What if the phone was bugged? If I used it to call a plumber, whoever was listening would rush over and grab me.

Because I needed clothing, quickly I threw socks, shirts, and pants into a carry bag. I also took a jacket, a pair of dress casual shoes, and a pair of sneakers. I left the house unlocked after my hasty exited. The plumber and furnace man I would phone later would need to get inside. I would tell them to lock up after they finished. As for when I would return, well, someone was after me. I might not be back. Ever. The thought was colder than the inside of my house.

Chapter 22
The Deco

After my encounter with Suzi, my perusal of the outsides of Jimmy's bar and residence, and the cold and wet message I received at my home, I panicked a little. Okay, more than a little. I did a lot of looking over my shoulder and into the rearview mirror as I drove into the city and stayed at a different hotel every night, paying in cash and registering under phony names. During the day, I searched for secure housing that would meet my needs. When I did not use my car, it was in a secure downtown garage but not in the same garage consecutive nights. I tipped the garage attendant at each place to let me know if anyone came snooping after me.

Before long, I found a combination of security and anonymity I in the Gold Coast. It was in the form of a furnished one-bedroom unit in The Deco at Lake Shore Drive and Schiller. Once a luxury hotel, it was a high rise rental building which offered the security of a 24-hour doorman and cardkey entry between 9 p.m. and 6 a.m. The Deco did not have a parking garage, but the high rise across Schiller had one with a 24-hour attendant and egress on both sides of the building. Renting an apartment and an indoor parking space was expensive, but I could afford it thanks to the late Jimmy.

For reasons I can't explained, living at The Deco cooled me out. No sooner did I check in than my anxiety began to check out.

My thinking changed, too, and I began to ask myself questions. Just why was I on the run? If tough guys were looking for me, they'd have found me. Shutting off my furnace was kid stuff compared to what wise guys would have done. My home would have been ransacked. Walls and ceilings would have been broken into and carpets and floorboards would have been ripped up during their search for Jimmy's money. My pursuers were a gorgeous former co-worker from B.O. High and someone in an Orange Car. What could they do to me, call the fashion police?

Panic was why I'd gone on the lam, and quite suddenly my panic was over. If someone wanted to approach me in a Dunkin Donut about the money or anything else, the next time they could buy me coffee. No sooner did I sign a lease at The Deco did I decided to return home where whoever wanted the money could ring my doorbell and ask for it.

Therein lie a problem. Not pertaining to the money, but to the returning home: my house still needed repairs.

I had made arrangements for a contractor to pump out the water and repair the water pipe and furnace. That work had been completed, but during our post-repairs phone conversation, the contractor informed me that because of the water damage and mold, some walls and flooring had to be torn out and replaced. Ugh. I had not thought of that. Did he knew of a construction company who could perform the work? Of course, he did. His brother-in-law is a construction contractor. I phoned him, and we made arrangements for his company to complete the repairs. The estimated completion date: two months. In conjunction, I had a locksmith change all of my locks and install an alarm system. The contractor was given the keys to my house and the alarm code, and the alarm was connected to the local police station. Whatever my insurance did not cover would have to be on Jimmy.

Regarding my new life in the Gold Coast, I enjoyed it while not letting down my guard completely. If I did not do so in everyday life, why would I do so in my new situation? So I made it a point to know all of the doormen at my new residence, their days and shifts. I greeted them whenever I entered or exited, and I made small talk with them. Occasionally I slipped them a few bucks, though not so much as to call attention to myself. I practiced the same with the valets who worked at the garage across the street. Without asking the service employees to do so, by ingratiating myself with them, I made them my eyes and ears.

I would not have to ask if anyone had arrived at the building asking about me. They would tell me everything I needed to know without my having to ask. I was gregarious and enjoyed meeting people, conversing with them. And of course in Cook County, if you paid someone, especially if they were in the service industry or had a government job, they believed owed you their allegiance. So it was good business.

Chapter 23
What Are the Odds?

Late one weeknight when I didn't feel like sleeping, I walked over to Mother's on Division Street, sat at the bar, and ordered a beer. The joint wasn't crowded. There was an NBA playoff game on one TV and a West Coast baseball game on another. I'd just taken my first sip when I heard a squeak. It wasn't a mechanical sound from a machine or a piece of furniture. The squeak came was a voice. I turned in its direction.

The Chihuahua was sitting on the stool next to me. Yet I was not caught off guard. I smiled and said the first thing that popped into my mind.

"What are the odds?"

The Chihuahua also was in good humor. She went along by giving cute little nod toward the TVs and saying, "If you're referring to one of those ball games, I've no clue. I'm not into gambling. A former boyfriend dabbled in it, but I don't get it. If you mean, my sitting down next to you, those odds are better. After I left B.O. High, I took a job downtown. I've lived in this neighborhood since."

"Beer?" I asked.

She politely shook me off. "I'm not a beer drinker." She turned toward the bartender and told him, "An orange thunder."

My cash was on the bar next to my drink. When the bartender returned with her drink, I pointed at it. "Out of here."

I picked up my beer. She did the same with her orange thunder. Spontaneously but lightly we touched glasses and drank.

"To your specifications?" I asked.

"Always. Expect less, receive less. Don't you find that to be true?"

I laughed a little at that because it was surprising to hear and profoundly true. "It's so basic. Yet I never thought about it until recently."

"Oh? Did something happen?"

I shrugged and explained, "A lot of somethings. Change of jobs, for one."

There was genuine surprise in her voice when she asked, "You're no longer working at B.O.? I did not know. All good, I hope."

I had to think about how to explain it. "Well, I abruptly decided to move on to something else. Recently I've begun to wonder if I should go back."

The Chihuahua looked into my eyes and quoted, "He had learned some of the things that every man must find out for himself, and he had found out about them as one has to find out – through error and through trial, through fantasy and illusion, through falsehood and his own damn foolishness . . ."

"How many times have you read that novel? I mean, to have memorized it."

The Chihuahua smiled proudly. "Once."

"You read *You Can't Go Home Again* only once, and you were able to memorize passages?"

She smirked and shrugged. "The gift of photographic memory. They tell me my paternal grandfather also had it. Anyway . . ."

"After hearing you recite that, I may have to move on," I quipped.

The smirk disappeared. She explained seriously, "I did. Moved on, that is. After my experience with B.O., I was upset. No, I was angry. People there started rumors. There were lies about me. Hell, I did them a favor by teaching P.E. and coaching the JV cheerleaders, two things I know nothing about yet did them well, and that was how they paid me off. I double majored in English and Art History, by the way."

She concluded, "Life was telling me it was time to move on, and I did. No regrets. Here I am."

"In a legendary Division Street bar sipping an orange thunder. You've done well."

She raised her glass. "Right back at ya."

She added, "How's this for a small world? Two of our former colleagues also live here?"

Of all I had seen and heard, that tidbit most caught me off guard. "Who?"

"Suzi and my former cheer partner, Gretchen. They live maybe two and a half blocks from here on Dearborn."

"What? I had gone from surprise to shock. "How do you know that?"

"Before I found my place, I looked at units in that neighborhood. I saw them going in their building. It's 1420 N. Dearborn. A very nice high rise. They must do well."

"Are you sure they weren't just visiting?"

Oh, no. They live there. I was curious and checked in the lobby. Their names are listed in the directory."

This was not The Chihuahua I thought I knew from B.O. High. She seemed sharp and sophisticated. She quoted classic literature. For my purposes, she provided valuable information. She was an Art History and English double major. I thought back to where our conversation started, about odds. Of Suzi and The Great Dane, a.k.a. Gretchen, just happening residing in my neighborhood. The answer was zero.

"You know," I told her. "I might just look them up."

"Hey, I have no hard feelings. If I met up with them, I'd probably indict them for dinner."

Finally the real Chihuahua showed up. Who said you can't go home again?

Chapter 24
Reconnecting With Suzi

To most observers, it must have appeared Suzie and I might come to blows on Dearborn directly in front of where The Chihuahua told me she resided. Looking back on it, I didn't think it was a big deal, but I could see how people might be concerned. Our voices were raised. Accusations flew, as did more than a few expletives in our doozy of an argument.

We really did not mean some of the things we said, but it felt good to let off steam.

I am certain she didn't expect me to do so when she said I could "kiss her ass." After I informed her I might consider doing so, but I would have to see it first, her retort was one a beautiful woman could get away with.

"You should be so lucky."

I must admit things did become a tad bit heated when we discussed the money, about which Suzi still didn't have a clue as to the correct amount.

"If you turn over the hundred thousand dollars that you took from Jimmy's, you'll never see me again!"

That was followed by my accusation that she and The Great Dane had placed a tracking device on my car. It actually was more than an accusation. Three days after my drink with The Chihuahua, I had the valet in the parking garage wash my car. He found it and gave it to me. That was when I stormed over to Suzi's building – it was only a few blocks from mine – and rang her buzzer. Leaned on it, actually.

When she answered via intercom, I informed her that I was there discuss the tracking device she had stuck to the underside of my car and, given the opportunity, where I intended to stick it. That wasn't precisely true since I had not brought the device with me. By that time, it had moved on. Suzi didn't know that, but my challenge did motivate her to rush downstairs to confront me. After I walked outside, Suzie, hurling descriptive expletives, followed me.

"Did you learn those terms at Brentwood School or Harvard-Westlake?" I shot back. "Anderson School of Management must teach more professional ones."

Suzi narrowed her perfect eyebrows, asked who the hell I thought I was, told me that she had erred since I wasn't fit to kiss the derriere of anyone from Minot, North Dakota let alone Malibu, and she assured me that she had forgotten more than a pseudo intellectual like me ever would know. There was more, but I didn't process the minutia because by that time people were coming up to us on the street – we somehow ended up in the middle of Dearborn Street – to ask if everything was okay. I got the impression the cyclists and dog walkers wanted us to start belting each other. That wasn't going to happen, at least not on my end. Had Suzi decked me, which I may have deserved, I would not have hit her back. I put my hands up and turned one hundred eighty degrees one way and back while re-assuredly repeating to the people walking their dogs or who'd stopped their cars,

"Everything is cool. Just a lover's spat. Sorry, folks."

To which Suzi affixed me with a laser-like glare and said with icy sarcasm, "Really, Goober? You and me? Now who would believe that?"

I changed the subject. "Speaking of things unfulfilled, where is Gretchen?"

"What's that supposed to mean?" Suzie knew it was an odd question, and I could tell it bothered her that I asked it. Approximately an hour earlier, I'd gone to the Red Line station at Clark and Division and affixed the little black box to an L car. At that moment, Gretchen might be cursing and wondering how and why I was driving back and forth between 95th Street and Howard and making intermittent stops in between.

I did not tell Suzi that. She would learn of it out soon enough, sooner if she calmed down and phoned Gretchen. As for my location, it was time to change it. I had done what I came to do: confront Suzi and blow off steam. Regarding what unexpectedly had transpired – Suzi following me into the street and us having a loud disagreement - if someone who witnessed our exchange refused to buy my explanation and called the police, it would get embarrassing. I did not want to be taken into custody for a domestic disturbance and have CPD inadvertently learn my disagreement with a beautiful woman actually was about a small fortune stolen from a dead bookie. Yes, the possibility of the police finding this out was farfetched, as was the way I acquired the money. Why take a chance? I turned and began to walk down the street to my building. I had said everything I had to say. Blowing off steam can be freeing. I felt great.

Suzi wasn't done. Not by a long shot. She followed me.

"Stop! I'm not done with you!" she shouted to me. "You had better stop and settle this with me now! If you don't, it will be worse for you later!"

I'd been one-half a block ahead of her, but when I entered my building, Suzi was right behind me. I may have responded to her with an over-the-shoulder expletive as I walked past the doorman, who must have been so surprised by what he was witnessing that he didn't stop Suzi. I'm not sure he could have had he tried.

"Hey! Hey! Stop!" she called out as I used my fob to pass through the secure inside door. She grabbed the door before it closed and was at my heels as I walked toward the elevator. I turned to face her.

"Where in the hell do you think you are going?" It wasn't intended to be a funny question, but I said it with laugh.

I noticed that she was sweating a little and her chest was heaving slightly when she assured me. "With you! I getting the damned money! It's not your money! You will not be leaving my sight until I get it!"

We stepped inside the elevator. The doors closed.

"Your eyes are going to get really tired from staring at me, baby, because hell will freeze over before you get anything from me."

This turned out to be not exactly true. I'm not sure which one of us pressed the emergency stop button or who starting undressing who first since by that time, everything was pretty much simultaneous. Negotiations became much more agreeable at that juncture.

Chapter 25
Sex, Lies, and F.B.I. Agents

Endorphins are powerful. We were drinking beer as Suzi casually yet matter-of-factly explained to me that she and Gretchen were F.B.I. agents. This was so farfetched. At the same time, it was exciting. I loved it! Thus it became it completely plausible. What were the odds I'd ever have sex with a beautiful FBI agent? Some people had their versions of the American Dream, and I had mine.

What were the odds? Where had I heard that recently?

Suzi did admit that, no, she wasn't from California. Nor was she from North Dakota. She laughed about not knowing why she'd referenced Minot, and her laugh featured a snort that was cute and sexy. In a serious tone, she said she could not tell me where she was from for security reasons, and I nodded in agreement. She confided that as field agents in the fraud division, she and Gretchen had been sent to Chicago to investigate Jimmy, who had been fencing stolen art from around the world. Suzi apologized for not using "allegedly," as is protocol until someone has been convicted, but she was certain Jimmy was doing everything "the Bureau" suspected and more.

The Bureau! I loved the sound of that.

"Most major felons do what they do for the money," she explained. "They're not like the Walter White character, who over time became the stereotypical control freak-perfectionist. They're more like Saul Goodman. They don't care how what they want gets done as long as it gets done, and they get what they want, which is to be paid. You get it?"

She laughed. I did, too. The way she put it was funny.

Even more seriously, if that were possible, Suzi told me that she and Gretchen had been installed at B.O. High, because two vital members of Jimmy's operation worked there. One was the airport connection, and the other was the go-between. They never did learn the identity of the go-between. That was frustrating.

"Our going under cover at B.O. with the full cooperation of the State Board of Education, the local school board, and school administrators. That was how I knew about why you were fired. The principal and AP were concerned there could be repercussions if, during our investigation, betting with Jimmy also was discovered. That's actually why you quickly were forced to resign. The administration didn't care, then suddenly it had the potential to become embarrassing. You were caught in the crossfire, so to speak. Sorry about the school board member part.

"What I told you in Dunkin Donuts about getting your job back was true. If you change your mind, let me know," she added. "I can pull strings."

After she jumped out of bed, ran to the kitchen to get us each another beer and got herself situated back in bed and propped up on pillows, Suzi drank and explained that Larry, the assistant football coach who worked also at O'Hare Airport, was the shipping connection. It was why The Great Dane became the cheerleading coach. She needed to get close to little Larry to try learn how things transpired back and forth between he and Jimmy. According to Suzi, everything was going according to plan until Angela exhibited some behaviors that caused them both to be fired.

Who was Angela, I asked.

Suzi smiled. "Angela is the tart everyone called "The Chihuahua."

It was somewhat of a revelation. I hadn't remembered anyone referring to her by her real name.

"Little Angela perpetrated some things into which Gretchen was, what's the right term, dragged? Angela was going to be fired. So that things did not become suspicious, we asked the administration to fire Gretchen, too. After which I came in. To that point, I had been tailing

Jimmy and Ed. Gretchen and I simply exchanged notes and flip flopped assignments."

"So Gretchen never assaulted the athletic director?"

"Nah. Gretchen may appear mean, but she wouldn't hurt a fly."

"She had me fooled," I told her.

Suzi changed the subject.

"Is there anyone more loathsome than Ed? He is the most pathetic excuse for a human. Gretchen came back to our place so completely repulsed one day after surveilling him that she wondered aloud if she could get away with accidentally shooting Ed when we busted Jimmy's operation."

So much for wouldn't hurt a fly.

When Jimmy was murdered, everything was thrown up in the air, Suzi said. A big problem for them, she admitted with some exasperation, was that neither she nor her partner ever had been inside Jimmy's home. So they didn't know exactly what Jimmy had on hand or whether he kept stolen art there. Or precisely how much money he kept on hand.

That they'd not been inside Jimmy's was a revelation, and it was helpful.

Suzi explained that she and Gretchen suspected Jimmy made some very big scores just before he was murdered, but she also admitted they did not have any idea if money actually was taken from Jimmy's, and if it had been, by whom. If there were money, it could have been Ed, or it could have been yours truly, and it could have been ten thousand dollars or it could have been ten million. I was wearing my best poker face by the time Suzi told me that Gretchen was doing surveillance from her car when she saw me run out with something in large shopping bags. It was at that point I became a suspect, and it was why they tracked me to Burr Ridge. Suzi admitted they'd become a bit impatient by the time she confronted me at the Dunkin' Donuts

I asked Suzie if she knew who had shut off my furnace and drilled a small hole in a water pipe that caused my basement to flood.

"No idea. That's not the way the Bureau does things now. Plumbers was the Nixon Administration."

"Good one!" I said, and we both laughed.

Suzie my beautiful, sexy lover reverted back to FBI agent when she said, "Maybe it was whoever else knows you have the money. You do have Jimmy's money?"

"How are you and Gretchen enjoying Gold Coast living?" I asked.

Suzi said she Gretchen were enjoying living in the Gold Coast on the government's dime. "The restaurants!" she gushed. Then with total seriousness, Suzi informed me that she "truly and honestly had to know" if I actually had taken any money from Jimmy's. She assured me that if I had and turned it over to her, there would be no charges against me or repercussions of any kind.

She gave me a long, soft kiss, rubbed up against me and said, "Obviously, we've gone beyond the F.B.I. agent-suspect relationship. Suzi pulled herself closer to me. She looked me in the eyes. Her lips brushed ever so softly against mine when she whispered. "Once and for all, did you take any money from Jimmy's?"

I sighed and kissed her and pulled back just enough for us to look into each other's eyes. The eyes don't lie, and both the kiss and my response felt genuine.

"Not one penny," I assured her.

Chapter 26
Kaboom!

We did not have the follow-up sex known as "a doubleheader." That's when two people make love, take a breather or a nap, become re-invigorated, and have at it again. After I'd assured Suzi that I hadn't taken any money from Jimmy's, she just said, "Okay. That is what I needed to know." She got out of bed and began getting dressed. I didn't want to get up. I just wanted to watch her.

She took a sexy deep breath, exhaled and smiled. "Well, this was unexpected and not unappreciated, and it sure as hell was a great diversion. Now I have to go back to work." She added with a look that indicated the appreciation of my sense of humor but the prospect of confronting and angry partner, "Gretchen will be returning to our place, livid, I'm sure, since you sent her on a wild goose chase from one side of town to the other. You put the tracking device under her car, didn't you?" Suzi smiled and shook her head. She was so smart. "Fortunately, you won't be crossing paths. We'll have to formulate a new plan now that we no longer have to follow you."

Suzi added facetiously, but I totally understood her meaning when she asked, "Do I have to make you raise your right hand and deputize you, or can I count on you not to talk to anyone about anything I told you? No one can know we're F.B.I. agents."

"Well, I am Goober," I reminder her.

"Okay, heat of the moment and sorry about that but seriously, we know little Angela is trolling the Gold Coast for no good reasons, but those reasons remain unknown to us. She is up to something, and Gretchen and I need to find out what asap. If you encounter her again, it's essential that you do not mention me, Gretchen, or our real occupations."

Suzi's intel was very good. I hadn't told her about my conversation with The Chihuahua at Cairo. How did she know? Because The Chihuahua found me, that made me wonder if she also suspected I had Jimmy's money and who she might be working with. Ed maybe? Or whoever Jimmy was fencing to or from? Hey. No problem. I assured Suzi she could count on me. By that time, she was fully dressed. She smooched me once more – a good one, not a one-night-stand-never-gonna-see-you-again kiss – and faster than I could say, "F.B.I., freeze." she was out of view in the living room and heading for the door. Suddenly her head appeared around the door frame, and she cautioned me, "That includes Gretchen. She can't find out that we, uh, you know."

I knew, and she knew I knew, which I guessed was why she quickly disappeared without receiving assurance. I heard the door to my place click closed. Wow. Was the D-Day Invasion that exciting? Then sound and the silence seemed to last forever.

Forevers can be finite. Mine lasted one day, at which time my curiosity, okay, and my need got the best of me, and I walked toward Suzi's place. I didn't know what I would do when I arrived there. I hoped I would see Suzi coming or going, and we could talk. Or something. It was noon on a beautiful late spring day. The sun was shining. Birds were chirping. The world seemed fresh and new.

I was approaching the building but still across the street and a few buildings north when I saw The Great Dane roar up in her Mercedes, screech it to a halt in a No Parking Zone across the street, which was maybe 100 feet in front of me. I know she did not see me. She wasn't looking in my direction when she jumped out and ran into their building. I'd froze in my spot when The Great Dane had pulled up, and I remained there and watched. If she was in that much of a hurry, something was up. Maybe she and Suzi would leave the building. I'd at least I'd get to see Suzi.

The Great Dane was inside for no more than three minutes when an explosion rocked the street and expelled a tongue of fire. It was followed by a huge cloud of black smoke and dust from the section of the high rise where Suzi's and The Great Dane's unit was. Particles of glass, wood, and mortar rained down on the street below. Through it, I could see flames and hear crackling inside the unit. Whoever was inside could not have survived the blast. For a long time, I just stood and watched. Looking up at the gaping hole that bellowed smoke from the front of 1410 N. Dearborn Parkway, I noticed that a fine layer of dust was settling onto the windshield of the cars.

People from other buildings came out into the street to find out what happened. Sirens screamed, first in the distance, then closer until first responders appeared on the street. Police and fire department units came to a halt in front of the building, leaped from their vehicles, and ran inside. More first responders arrived. People were evacuated from the building. I looked for Suzie and The Great Dane, but neither was among the evacuees.

The 1400 block of Dearborn quickly was closed at each end. TV trucks appeared, and because those vehicles couldn't access the street, men and women came running with cameras and microphones trailed by long black cords. A helicopter hovered overhead. As I watched the controlled chaos, I thought about how the media would explain the incident. There would be initial reports of a possible terrorist attack. Thereafter, depending upon what the media was fed, it would be reported that authorities were investigating the possibility that a gas leak precipitated the explosion. The Great Dane had to be dead. I hoped there would not be a report that more people were killed.

Either way, the real story would not ever come out, which I suspected was that someone achieved their goal. They blew Gretchen to bits and maybe Suzi, too.

That night, I had a late dinner at a restaurant on Wells Street. My destination was a straight shot west, but I walked out of my way to see Suzi's building. The street remained blocked to vehicle traffic, but pedestrian traffic was permitted, and gawkers stood, stared, and pointed from across the street. Police were stationed in front of the building so that no one got near it. And while 1410 N Dearborn was in surprisingly good shape on the outside. The contrast was the big black hole around where Suzi's and The Great Dane's unit had been. The building had a big black eye.

I stretched dinner into a few drinks at the bar afterward. Suzi had to be dead, and I was bummed I because I wouldn't see her again. I walked past her building again on the way home, but I did not linger. What could I possibly see? I returned to my own unit at about 12:30. I got out of my clothes, washed my face, brushed my teeth, and climbed into bed.

The alcohol I'd consumed must have helped. I was in bed only a few minutes before I fell asleep. Yet it wasn't a peaceful sleep. In my slumber, I was confronted by a ghost with a gun.

Chapter 27
Lying Low or Just Lying?

Suzie must have come out of the closet, and her re-emergence had nothing to do with sexual preference. The first thing I realized after I awoke from just a few minutes of sleep was that I was on my stomach and Suzie was on my back. She also was holding a small caliber handgun to my left ear.

I groaned. "I'm glad you're alive, dear, but not tonight. I have an earache."

Suzie sounded angry when she informed me, "Funny. Now tell me that you had nothing to do with our place blowing up."

I understood. Her friend and partner had been killed, and someone wanted her dead. If they knew she remained alive, they might come after her again. She had to determine who was responsible.

"Could it have been an accident?"

"Zero," Suzi informed me. "I spoke with the investigators. The explosion was caused by a timed device brought inside our unit."

"Do I seem to be the type to do something like that? Do I have that skills set? Creating an explosive device, breaking into your unit, and setting a timer. I'm a history teacher. I wasn't in the CIA or special forces."

I added, "If Jimmy's operation was as big as you suspect, someone connected to it could have come after you even if they didn't know you're FBI. They could just be out to eliminate anyone with knowledge of its existence."

To me, the silence that followed was too long. Finally I felt Suzi's body relax and the gun move from my head and drop onto the bed. Suzi rolled off of me and lay next to me, and our proximity did not invite intimacy. There was tension. I rolled over, and we lay on our backs a foot apart, staring at the ceiling in the dark bedroom. Suzi sighed in what must have been exasperation and exhaustion.

"Have you considered possible suspects?" I asked. "If not related to Jimmy's operation, someone with an axe to grind."

Suzi sounded like an F.B.I. agent when she said, "Anyone is capable of anything. At this point, I have no clue. If you have any ideas, well, let's say that no theory will be too farfetched. Someone blew up a unit in a secure luxury high rise building. It wasn't done on a whim. It was ballsy. It was planned, and the planners aren't lucky. They are very good at what they do."

"So more could follow," I said fully aware of the new reality.

"For me if they find out I survived, and for you, too, if this was connected to Jimmy."

"If you want my vote, Ed is involved. He had to know everything Jimmy was doing. They lived together. Ed was Jimmy's trusted stooge," I offered. "Jimmy was Ed's guarantee of an easy life. Besides money or stolen goods, Ed must be very angry at the prospect of going back to work on a garbage truck. The last thing he wants is to break a sweat."

"You tracked me. Did either you or Gretchen tail Ed?"

Suzi admitted they hadn't.

"Since Jimmy's death, I no longer believe in coincidences," I explained. "Ed was Jimmy's roomie and stooge. He found his body on the kitchen floor when he returned home after bartending. The end of la dolce vita had to bother him. Maybe he's looking for someone to blame. Why you, I have no idea."

"Ed is a total wanker," Suzi told me. "He is mean and angry enough to do something like that, but he'd have to have help. Ed is not the type to plan out anything."

Suzi was right, and I told her so. "No question he could not work alone."

She blew me away with what she asked next.

"Did Jimmy offer to hire you to do anything pertaining to the stolen art, such as researching some of the pieces or determining actual values?"

"How do you know that?"

"I'm paid to know that and lots more. Now here's what else you need to know. Bookmaking always was one of Jimmy's side businesses, and it was a small moneymaker. The bar business was small, too, but that was the vehicle to launder money. Further back, when Jimmy was with the beer distributor, we suspect he was behind a series of warehouse thefts. When he moved to the phone company, he was into stolen communications equipment."

"Where is this history lesson going?"

"Each time, just before law enforcement was about to bust him, he hired an unsuspecting front. He paid the guy a lot of money and got him involved just enough to take the rap."

"After they were arrested, why didn't they blow the whistle on Jimmy and his operation? Wouldn't they testify?"

"Couldn't."

I hit me like slap in the face. "Oh, no."

"All the evidence pointed to them when they disappeared. Each was found weeks afterward, one in a landfill another in the trunk of a car in a salvage yard. You get the idea."

"But nothing to pin the raps on Jimmy or Ed?"

"Nope."

"Jimmy must have had other people working in his organization. Not schmucks like Ed, but crafty people who can create fronts, scenarios, and alibis. Will you help me find out who they are and who killed my partner?"

"Are you serious? The other day when you mentioned swearing me in, you were joking. Now . . ."

"Now things are different. Tomorrow Gretchen's death will be reported by the media. Not by name. Nor will the detail that she was an F.B.I. agent. It will be along the lines of, "Two women were killed in the blast. Their identities are being withheld pending notification of the victim's families."

I'd heard enough explosions reported by the media to add, "It also will be announced that you were killed in the explosion. Not by name. Let me guess. The explosion will be attributed to a gas leak. I could say, 'The poor Gas Company always is blamed.' Except for one thing. It gets revenge by raising our rates.

"Scapegoating could be a line item on the monthly utility bills." Seriously, Suzi added. "It informs the public no one is in danger and everyone gets some form of closure. Hopefully the perpetrators, if they believe I'm dead. If they do, they won't know we're looking for them."

"Now we're a 'we'?"

"The Bureau told me to lay low. To remain out of sight. So officially I'm on hold," she explained. "Except my partner has been killed, and I'm not close to wrapping up this case. I can't sit around and wait for something to happen. I'm going to solve this. You can help me, and I can keep you close to me. They came after me. I'm worried they might come after you."

At that point in our conversation, I no longer was scared; I was frisky. I moved my body closer to hers. "We are pretty good together. Will there be other collaborations?"

Suzi did not react to my signal. "That's just about all I have."

"Just about?"

Up to that point, we'd been in bed without any significant contact until a few second prior, and we'd been talking straight up at the ceiling. Finally Suzi moved closer and turned toward me. Her lips were close to mine.

"Okay, I need you. Does that help?" Suzi told me sincerely. "We'll have tonight and tomorrow. Beyond that is a maybe."

"What about *The New York Times* Crossword Puzzle?"

"Oh, we'll always have that."

That was it. She had me. "What will be on the agenda for tomorrow?"

"We're going to find Ed."

Suzi got out of bed. She began to undress. As she did so, I propped myself up on my elbows and watched. "Under the circumstances, it's impossible for me to say no."

Suzi raised the covers and climbed into bed next to me. We shifted toward each other. We kissed, and I whispered to her, "I will help you under one condition."

Suzi pulled away from me in surprise. "What condition? I can't sign anything or give you a badge."

I held up the gun I had rolled over onto. "Can we get this out of the bed?"

Chapter 28
Grandma's Furniture and an Open Door

Suzie and I didn't make love. We were exhausted. The closest we came to quality physical contact was some spooning and an intermittent arm drape or leg lock. The gun spent the night on the dresser.

We rose at ten, took turns showering, and prepared to go out and locate Ed. Suzie wore some of her clothes from the night before: jeans and sneakers. I loaned her shorty socks, t-shirt, baseball cap, and a sports coat I'd recently purchased and which she cuffed up the sleeves and looked really cute in. She'd brought the essential under-30 accessory: sunglasses. With the shades and the ball cap, she didn't look like Suzi, but she did look like the woman who didn't want to be bothered but who was so cool and so beautiful that no one could help staring at her. What if someone staring at the hot chick wearing shades and a ball cap stared long and hard enough to realize it was the woman whose living space and roommate had been blown to smithereens? Or what if someone recognized me as the guy who had argued with that woman on the street outside of a high rise building that later blew up?

That potential recognition problem quickly was resolved. Suzi had put the finishing touches on her appearance in the bath room. I'd done so in the bedroom. We happened to exit our locations simultaneously and met face-to-face in the hallway between. We reviewed each other up and down and began to laugh.

Suzi removed the cap and shook out her hair. "We're the epitome of the Gold Coast. That makes us a cliché. I can't imagine us confronting anyone in these getups, even someone as cartoonish as Ed. Who could take us seriously?"

I added, "Then we shouldn't risk hitting a breakfast place like Tempo or the Pancake House. It would be asking for someone from the neighborhood to recognize us as and call the cops. Or worse, the media."

"I could get us out of anything with law enforcement, but it still would be a waste of our time. The media would lead to a slew of bigger problems, the worst of which being our covers would be blown."

"We don't need to go out. I have provisions," I suggested.

Suzi seconded. "A much better plan. It makes more sense to spend the day here and pay Ed a visit after dark." He paused in thought. "It seems we have some time to kill. Suggestions?"

My suggestion to while away the hours was simple.

"Let's back to bed."

Without another word, Suzi walked past me into the bedroom. She was undressing as she did.

Hours later we got out of bed and dressed again, this time in outfits we thought more functional. We did not shower again. In this Suzie and I shared a philosophy, and it was one more reason she had become so incredibly attractive for reasons that exceeded her beauty.

I broiled burgers, and Suzi made scrambled eggs mixed with fresh veggies. We ate everything. We drank coffee. We discussed how we would go about finding and approaching Ed. By the time we finished eating and strategizing, it was late afternoon.

Local TV news began at 4 p.m. That was when I turned on the TV. Suzi took the remote control and flipped from one local newscast to another until we heard, as she had predicted, the same story from all four news sources. The preliminary report from Chicago Fire Department investigators indicated a gas leak inside a unit caused the explosion in a high rise on the 1400 block of North Dearborn. The two women who rented the unit were killed in the blast. Their identities were not released pending notification of family members. According to city inspectors, the building is structurally safe, and except those displaced due to damage caused by the explosion or collateral water damage, residents of units inspected and determined inhabitable may return.

We watched local news until 5:30 when Suzi flipped it to national news. At that point, we were killing time waiting for dusk. We took turns using the bathroom to brush our teeth and freshen up. By 6:30, anxiousness in the form of nervous energy took over, and Suzi said, "Let's go." We went out the door and down to the parking garage. The valet retrieved my car. I noticed Suzi was careful not to go near him. She'd donned her sunglasses before stepping off to the side to wait during my interaction with him and the process of delivering the car. He wasn't oblivious to Suzi, however. After delivering it, he was going to get the door for her. I politely waved him off.

"Oh, don't bother. I've got it," I told him as I extended my right hand with some bills. He took them, thanked me, and stepped aside. As though she'd done it before, head lowered and face turned away from him, Suzi ducked inside the passenger seat. I closed the door, and hurried into the driver seat. The garage door opened automatically whenever a car approached from the inside. I buckled in, shifted the car into gear, and stepped on the gas.

Finally we were out the door and down the street. Yet we were in no hurry. Darkness would be our ally. The darker the better. Dusk had settled in, and we were at least an hour from where we needed the night to be. As we took our time on the drive south, Suzi brought me up to speed on the investigation.

"Jimmy was the big fish. When he was killed, the F.B.I. investigation shifted to trading partners. Ed and Angela were considered little fish."

"So The Chihuahua was involved with Jimmy?" I was surprised.

"Not directly," Suzi explained. "She was incorporated by the guy from B.O. High, Larry, who worked at the airport. She was a low-level runner. I don't know if she had dealings with Jimmy or every met him.

Suzi added, "Ultimately, they'd have been pinched when Jimmy was indicted. The F.B.I. did not take them too seriously. The philosophy is not to waste time and resources on the mice. Go after the elephants. The Bureau figured they would be swept up and flip on Jimmy to get light sentences."

I glanced a Suzie so I could gauge her reaction after I said, "The F.B.I. screwed up. It underestimated them and their roles with Jimmy's organization. One or both of them blew up your place and killed your partner. Flunkies don't do that after the boss is killed. They lay low or disappear."

Suzi did not take offense at my rebuke of the F.B.I. On the contrary, she was unfazed. Suzi appeared comfortable and confident in the passenger seat when she said to me, "No doubt in my mind that Ed was involved. We'll have a better picture of to what extent when we find him.

She reminded me, "We are not going to grab him or even confront him. We're just going to find out what he's up to, see if he's at the bar, or still living at Jimmy's. That will give me more to go on when I return to active duty."

Which to Suzi Chen was no more than a mere designation. Were it not, she wouldn't be going after Ed, and she would not have incorporated yours truly.

We arrived at Jimmy's just after nine. It was dark enough. Jimmy lived on a tree-lined street, which was more advantageous for us. It was not too dark, however, for us to see the real estate sign that said "SOLD."

Suzi said, "The uncle is the closest living relative. I did not receive information that he was out on bond. Even if he were, I don't think he legally could put the house on the market."

I added, "Jimmy hasn't been dead long enough for everything to be processed. Even if he had a living will, a trust, whatever. It would take what, six months minimum? My grandmother had a living will. After she passed, it took her attorney eight months to distribute the property and assets to the heirs."

Suzi shot me a knowing look and asked, "Did you get anything?"

"Grandma had a beautiful antique buffet and accompanying dining room table and chairs. You would think that one of her children would want that beautiful set, but no one did. Everyone had their own dining room furniture and was happy with what they had. Come the day grandma's house was cleared out, guess who gets a call?

"The movers were there, but the buffet, the table, and the chairs didn't have a destination. Cousins designated to get them reside out of state. They were supposed to drive in with a truck, but they didn't show up. Grandma's children were not going to pay movers to deliver the stuff to them, and they weren't going put Grandma's furniture on the parkway. We're frugal and practical. Call it a family tradition."

"Putting Grandma's furniture on the parkway for anyone to take would have haunted them the rest of their lives. Grandma probably would have haunted them, too," Suzi joked. "So you made out."

"I made out. To that point, my dining room furniture was, well, let me just say it was not of high quality. So unless I eventually married someone with taste . . ."

Suzi shook her head and gave a slight wag of her right index finger. "That's a given. You weren't at the stage of life where you would make that type of purchase. Eventually you would have." She was being magnanimous, not correcting or condescending, and I was appreciative.

"Exactly," I said."

We had been sitting in my car looking out at Jimmy's house, which was dark. The street was dimly lit by street lights and scant moonlight that could seep through slightly swaying tree branches. As suddenly the conversation about inheritances was over, Suzi opened the passenger side door and began to exit the car. That surprised me. Before she was all the way out, I leaned toward her and whispered with urgency, "Where are you going?"

"To look around the outside of Jimmy's and through the windows."

"You're not worried that anyone will see you snooping around a murder victim's home?"

"No one will see us if they don't see the interior car light, take a closer look, and notice two people having a conversation inside. Now get your grandma's antique furniture saving ass out here."

So much for understanding. Suzi closed the door and walked toward Jimmy's. I smirked, exited the car, and followed. By the time I caught up with Suzi, she was all the way up the walk near the front door.

"Where in the hell are you going," I whispered with the same urgent tone. It hadn't deterred Suzi the first time. Why did I think it would work the second?

"I am going to try the front door."

"What if it's open?" I asked as she walked toward the door. The answer came shortly. It was. As I watched, Suzi opened it and walked inside. For what seemed to be an eternity, I remained frozen where I stood. Finally the door opened, Suzi's head popped out, and she said, "Don't go Barney Fife on me. Get in here."

Against my better judgement, I entered.

The living room drapes were closed, which made the inside of the house darker than outside. I said, "I wish I'd have thought to bring a flashlight."

No sooner were the words out of my mouth than there was light, and it momentarily blinded us. When our eyes recovered, we saw Ed standing at a light switch with a gun pointing at us.

"I got 'em! he called toward the kitchen. A moment later, a light was turned on in that part of the house.

Ed stepped to the side and motioned with the nose of the gun. "Walk that way. You'll be walkin' toward another gun. So don't try nuttin' funny. It wouldn' take much for wunna us to put a coupla pills inta youz."

Chapter 29
When Following Ed Is a Good Idea

Suzi and I exchanged shoulder shrugs and we-have-no-choice looks before we followed Ed's command. Suzi appeared unfazed and went first. Scared down to my socks, I followed her. Ed brought up the rear. He didn't need to jab the gun into my back as motivation since I was moving. So I suspect he did it because besides being a hater, he was a sadist. Past the smirking orange-haired nude we went. When we arrived in the kitchen, we saw The Chihuahua seated on a stool at one of the islands. She didn't have a gun. The Chihuahua stood up and said, "Nice work, Ed."

Seeing The Chihuahua triggered something in my memory, but I didn't get to complete the thought because Suzi snarled at her, "So you *were* working together!"

The Chihuahua smiled broadly. "Always. Working together and working *with* someone," she replied with equal emphasis. "Ta da!" she announced, and she hopped off of the stool, raised her arms, and then extended them toward the back hallway.

On cue, Jimmy stepped from the back hallway into the light of the kitchen.

"Jimmy," Suzi spat out his name. "I cannot say I am surprised."

I was, and I said so. "What the hell, Jimmy! You were dead! I saw you lying on the kitchen floor!"

"I was, almost, and thanks for callin' 9-1-1 when ya foun' me," he said sarcastically. "Had Angela not arrived after ya left, I wouldn' be here." He walked over, bend slightly, and threw his arms around The Chihuahua. She looked up at him. Jimmy leaned down, and they kissed. It was absolutely repulsive.

"She found you," I said. "According to the newspaper, it was Ed."

"Let's just say it was more convenient that way," Jimmy told me.

"I had just parked on the street when you were leaving with the bags full of money. I ran inside and found Jimmy."

"You have an orange car," I said. It was more thinking aloud than to The Chihuahua. The light bulb slowly was going on but there was no joy or relief that it finally had. "You ordered an orange thunder when we just happened to meet on Division Street."

Again my train of thought was interrupted, this time by Jimmy. He shot me a nasty look, and, his bushy eyebrows so menacingly narrow they seemed to form a V above his eyes. He growled, "I hope ya didn' spen' anya dat money."

I didn't think Jimmy could be more upset than he was, and I didn't know if it mattered at that point. I whispered to Suzi, "You told me you saw me running out of here."

"Focus," Suzi whispered back, "Don't start buying into this."

I wasn't sure if Jimmy heard us, but our body language and demeanors were enough for him to interject. He nodded toward Suzi, but he started with me. "Oh, she didn't tell ya everything?" He shifted his stare to Suzi. "What a surprise." To both of us, he said, Unfortunatley, dere's no time for who Suzi really is an' how we became associated. We need ta fine out where da money is cuz dat's gonna determine how things 'r gonna go for youz an' whedda we have ta hoit ya."

I didn't like that Jimmy added the possibility of hurt, but Suzi was remained unfazed. She ignored Jimmy and resumed on the little woman whose arms were wrapped around as much of Jimmy's immense waste as they could be.

"The Chihuahua," she said with derision. "I should have known you had something to do with Gretchen's death."

The Chihuahua pulled away from Jimmy's huge belly just long enough to huffily respond, "I prefer Angela."

"How about sociopathic nymphomaniac?"

Jimmy snapped his fingers at Ed, and Ed turned the gun directly on Suzi. She didn't flinch, but I did. I put up my arms and stepped in front of her. "Whoa. Let's everybody tone down the rhetoric and get back to what's most important. For you, it's recovering money. For us, it is staying alive. Let's negotiate."

"Negotiate. Ha. Dat's a good one," Jimmy chuckle growled, and as he did, his belly bounced. So did The Chihuahua, who smiled contentedly. It would have been comical had our lives not been on the line.

Suzi's bravado continued to impress me and alarm me. She said, "If we're going to be killed by a sadistic nobody and an indiscriminate nymphet, I'd like to at least know what happened. First, however, to you, Jimmy, kudos. You've always been a genius when it came to taking advantage of a situation. You didn't plan to fake your death. Now you seem poised to use it to your advantage. Is that right"

The other two were not oblivious to the insults. The anger that flashed across Ed's face made it obvious he wanted to shoot Suzi on the spot, and The Chihuahua bared her incisors. As always, Jimmy was in control, and he'd been flattered. Feeling magnanimous, he raised an index finger of intercession to Ed. To Suzi, he huffed and said, "Won't do ya no good, but go ahead. Whaddaya got?"

Suzi smiled at Jimmy before she began. It was a knowing smile. She said, "The heat was on your fencing operation. You were concerned about being charged with crimes that ranged from money laundering to income tax evasion. The government can't charge a dead man. Was that your thinking?"

"Pretty much. I'd been considerin' options for my escape, but I couldn't come up da poific one. Den my uncle comes over askin' ta borrow money – dere was no friggin way *dat* was gonna happen - and whacks me onna backa da head wid a skillet. I hit da floor. I'm almost dead. Had lil' Angela not come over an' foun' me, I mighta been dead.

She called Ed, and he tol' her whata do over da phone. Den he rushed home from da bar ta make sure I was gonna be okay."

Ed interjected, "I was a paramedic in Afghanistan."

"Oh, yeah? Whose side," I said.

Ed turned the gun on me. "Lemme blast 'im, Jimmy!"

"Not yet, Ed. I'm not finished. You can shoot 'im later. I promise." To me, he said, "The only thing saved ya, teacher, is I promised gorgeous here ta answer her questions. Now les continue." Jimmy smile and added, "I'm enjoyin' dis."

I wasn't, and Ed wasn't completely placated, but he had to settle for putting a hole through me with his stare and sinister smile.

Jimmy said to me. "An' by da way, did youz really think you was gonna walk outta here wid half a million dollars cash 'n get ta keep it?"

Suzi whispered to me. "So it was half a million?" She sounded more impressed than surprised.

I shook my head. To Suzi I whispered, "Didn't you just warn me not to buy in?" I cleared my throat and told Jimmy, "Not me."

Suzi smirked at me and informed Jimmy, "Nor me."

Jimmy looked at me then at Suzi. "Yeah, right. Coupla innacents."

Suzi moved him off the sore spot of the money when she said, "Getting back to your story, what happened next? Your death was reported by the media. Law enforcement confirmed it publicly. You must have paid off officials fairly high up the hierarchy."

"Da right people," Jimmy corrected her and emphasized, "Ya gotta pay da right people. Even if it costs a few more bucks, it ties up all possible loose ends. Couple of 'em already owed me favors. They gambled with me, and I was holdin' a few markers. You get da idea."

Jimmy concluded, "Anyway, yeah. Da fix went in. Take no chances. Dat's my motto."

"Suzi interjected, "Let me guess. You paid an attorney to create a trust – post mortem - that in the event of your untimely demise, which already had occurred, Ed and little Angela here control of everything. The bar, the house, all of your assets."

Jimmy had a smug look on his face. He shrugged and nodded. I sensed he was beginning to lose focus, which would not be good for us. We needed him to keep talking. I jumped in. "And just like one of those cable TV shows in which the main character needs to disappear, you have someone lined up to create a new identity for you."

Jimmy responded the way I hoped he would.

"Good one, history teacher. Yeah. Dere's a guy named Louie operates a currency exchange on east 79th Street in Englewood. I got to know him when I worked for da phone cumpnee. Louie's a sharp guy. Got his start working for da Cook County Clerk. Knows all da ins n' outs, all 'bout records 'n how ta change ol' ones 'n create new ones. His real money-makin' bidness is sellin' new identities. No questions asked and complete discretion. He's created new identities fer da tree a us fer when we disappear. Louie don' know where we're going. Relocation ain't parta da package. He doesn't wanna know. Doesn' care. Ain't his business. His bidness is gettin paid."

"You died, and you are going to live happily ever after," Suzi marveled in admiration. "Oh, that's good. That is very, very good."

"No, it's great," Jimmy corrected her and added, "Since we first began doin' bidness ta'gether, I suspected ya underestimated me." He shrugged before concluding. "I never took it personal, but looka where you are and where I am."

Suzi agreed. "Well, I never expected to wind up on the wrong end of a gun." She added, "Hey, how did you find out where Gretchen and I lived?"

"Dat was all Angela's doin'." He looked down at The Chihuahua. She looked up. They leaned into each other, hugged, and kissed. It was comical and repulsive.

Suzi asked her, "How did you do it? I thought we covered our tracks pretty well."

The Chihuahua grinned and told her. "I didn't find you. I found him." She nodded at me. "We always suspected he took the half million dollars from here, and you two would go after it. So find him, and he leads us to the money and to you."

Suzi winced and said, "You put a tracker on his car."

The Chihuahua said acidly. "Oh, you thought you were the only one who knew that trick?"

Jimmy jumped in. "I worked for da phone company, remember? In da old days, it was eaves dropping by listnin' in on phone conversations and tapping phones. Today it's 'lectronics dat include trackin'. Anyway, yeah, I still got contacts dere."

The lightbulb went on for me. I said to Suzi, "It was a red herring. The valet at my building didn't find the tracking device you placed under my car. He was paid to show it to me." To The Chihuahua, I said, "You paid off the valet, andh put your device under my car."

The Chihuahua didn't respond, but Suzi did, and it was to me.

"When you learned about the tracker, you became angry and stormed over to my place," Suzi told me.

The Chihuahua laughed and said, "It was like waving a flag in front of a Red Bull."

I was about to comment on the malapropism when Suzi held up her hand at me like a stop sign. "Don't. We're almost there," she told me. To The Chihuahua and Ed, she said, "Which of you followed him?"

Ed answered. "What you really want to know is which of us blew up your place?"

Suzi nodded. "That is precisely what I need to know."

Ed told her, "It was me. I posed as the cable guy to get into the building. After I got inside, the rest was easy."

"Killing my partner was easy?"

Ed shrugged a no-big-deal acknowledgement. "Yeah.

It was all Suzi needed to hear. She pulled a gun and shot him.

Chapter 30
Lock 'Em In the Basement

Instantly I understood two things: the weapon was the same one Suzi'd previously stuck into my ear, and Ed had not received military police or special forces training. He had done a lousy job of frisking Suzi. As a thank you, Suzi shot the gun out of his hand.

There wasn't time to celebrate Suzi's cunning or marksmanship. While Ed was squeezing his bleeding hand, jumping up and down in pain, and cursing loudly, I ran over and picked up the gun he'd dropped. For the first time in my life, I had a gun in my hand. It felt funny, but the sensation did not stop me from pointing the weapon at our three shocked captives.

"Why didn't you tell me you brought the gun?" I asked. I was so happy that I held my right hand out and up for Suzi to slap me a high five.

Suzi slapped my outstretched hand and said, "Didn't think you needed to know. I had it in the butt of my jeans. I knew we would need it, and figured that if Ed got the drop on us, he wouldn't frisk me. Ed's a misanthrope. He hates interacting with people. There is no way he is going to touch one." To Ed, Suzi said, "Your insecurities finally did you in. What do you think about that, Eddie baby?"

Suzi's comments cause Jimmy to curse Ed, Ed to curse Suzi, and The Chihuahua to squeal. That caused Suzi and I to shift our weapons back and forth at each of them. Suddenly we were two jumpy cops on their first bust.

"Let's keep our guns on them from different angles," I suggested, and as I did so I stepped back and away from Suzi. "Now even if one of our guns accidentally goes off, we'll hit Moe, Larry, or Shirley and not each other."

"You ain't got no reason ta use doze guns," Jimmy said in his most reasonable growl. "I got money an' artwork here. We kin make a deal."

Suzi's eyes narrowed. "Fatty, I'm going to give all of you the same deal you gave Gretchen."

Jimmy gasped at Suzi's pronouncement, and The Chihuahua yelped and scurried to hide behind him. Ed winced in silence as he dripped blood onto the kitchen floor.

Suzi told The Chihuahua, "You, dog breath. Go over to the sink and get Ed a towel before he loses a quart onto the linoleum."

The Chihuahua was completely terrified. No one had noticed before Suzi had spoken to her, but at some point in the festivities The Chihuahua had wet herself. Yellow drops fell from her pelvic area as though there were a leaky faucet under her skirt. There was a puddle on the floor where she stood, and it had begun to smell.

Suzi said in mock sympathy, "Aww. You've had an accident. That's too bad." She stepped forward, stuck the gun into The Chihuahua's face, and sternly said, "Get a towel. Wrap it around Ed's hand. Then get another towel and wipe up your mess. Do it now."

There had been rumors The Chihuahua responded well to things long, hard, and glistening. She let go of Jimmy, scooted to a drawer at the sink, opened it, and grabbed two dish towels. With her eyes on the gun Suzi had pointed at her, she moved quickly to Ed and wrapped his hand in one of the towels. Ed grimaced but didn't bother to thank her, and The Chihuahua didn't wait for gratitude. She scurried over to where she'd created a puddle, crouched, and hurriedly wiped it dry with the other towel. When she was done, she stood up and looked at Suzi, who motioned with the gun to the sink. The little woman understood. She walked to the sink, dropped the urine-soaked towel into it, and hurried back to her Jimmy's side.

Suzi was just warming up. She said, "Now you, fatty, you're going to get the money you mentioned, and it better be equal to or greater than the amount you chiseled out of Gretchen and me. Where is it?"

Jimmy seemed to quiver for a moment – his jowls shook – before he composed himself and motioned for Suzi to follow. "Dis way," he told her.

"Chiseled?" I asked Suzi.

She shook her head and made a sour face. "It was a cover. I'll explain later."

Gun raised, Suzi nodded and stepped toward Jimmy. She said to me before she and Jimmy disappeared into another room, "If you hear anything that sounds suspicious, don't hesitate. Shoot them both." At this, The Chihuahua yelped. Ed, still nursing his hand, may have been going into shock. He simply stood there holding his bleeding hand.

Jimmy and Suzi weren't gone long, probably no more than three minutes. Jimmy re-appeared first, and he was carrying a small suitcase. Suzi with the gun in his back followed him into the kitchen. She told Jimmy, "Set the suitcase atop the nearest counter and walk back to where you were standing." Jimmy did so, and Suzi said to me, "Watch them while I open the suitcase."

Suzi stepped the case. With her free hand, she unlatched the case. As she did that and inspected the contents, her eyes went back and forth between us and what was inside. She closed the case and stepped back to where she'd stood.

"Money?" I asked.

"And a lot of it," she replied. There was an unexpected emotion in her voice: relief.

"Dat gonna buy our freedom?" he asked Suzi.

She shook her head. "Not quite," she told him. "Strip. All three of you."

Jimmy and Ed stared at Suzi as though she'd been speaking a foreign language. The Chihuahua began peeling off her clothing as though it were the most natural thing in the world. When she was through, the lightbulb went on for me.

The lightbulb finally burned brightly. I exclaimed to her, "You're the woman in the portrait in the living room!"

She nodded proudly and smirked. It was the same smirk. Just as proudly, Jimmy said, "I painted it."

"You?" I said. "No way."

Jimmy set me straight. "Art always came natural ta me. I always jus' got it, and it was the only thing I was good at in school. Whydya think I went inta da stolen art bidness? I like I art, an' I get it. Duh."

Suzi interjected, "And it's profitable."

Jimmy admitted. "Dat, too."

"Now back to the business at hand. You and Ed. Clothes off. Now. Or so help me, I will shoot you both."

Jimmy looked at The Chihuahua, and she nodded, but he still didn't appear persuaded, and Ed wasn't budging. Suzi told them, "Do you two have a problem with nudity? After what you did to Gretchen, I don't need another reason to kill you both. Now strip or I will shoot you."

I broke the tension when I said, "Can't we just shoot them? I'd rather see them dead than naked."

I wasn't sure if Suzi took me seriously, or if she were running a bluff when she stepped toward Jimmy, raised the gun to the level of his eyes, and pulled back the hammer. It was chilling.

Jimmy didn't need another verbal command. His hands dropped to his belt, he unbuckled it, and his trousers dropped to his ankles. He told The Chihuahua. "Help Ed."

The Chihuahua looked at Suzi, and she nodded. The little woman stepped to Ed, unbuttoned his shirt, and helped him out of it. She unbuckled his trousers, and they slid to the floor. Ed kicked off his shoes. He wasn't wearing socks.

Much of the tension left the room. Suzi, more relaxed, stepped back. She said, "A wise decision, boys. Now all three of you kick your duds into one big pile in front of you."

We had the situation calm and under control, but I couldn't help ruin it. I started laughing.

"What's so damned funny?" Jimmy growled.

I almost couldn't stop laughing long enough to reply. I pointed to Jimmy's legs. "Those," I said. "I've never see such a skinny set of pins on that large a torso."

It wasn't so much a criticism as an observation. In addition to the pathetically skinny legs, Jimmy's immense belly hung so low that you couldn't see his genitals. It was as though someone put a pear atop two drinking straws.

"Mother Nature has a vivid imagination," agreed Suzi, "and sometimes a twisted sense of humor."

"The entire picture might be surrealism, but Jimmy's legs alone would be minimalism," I interjected and pointed to Ed. "Not that he's going to enter Mr. Universe."

Ed's legs also were pathetically skinny – he had no muscle tone, and he was pale – but they at least they were proportional to the rest of his emaciated frame. And Ed was vain, and vanity had priorities. He had taken the dish towel from his bleeding hand and used it to cover his genitals.

I was just about to provide commentary on Ed, when Jimmy provided a comeback. It was cold.

"What I got can't be too bad. Gretchen enjoyed it."

The Chihuahua glared at Jimmy upon hearing of his betrayal, but that was the least of his problems. Anger flashed across Suzi's face, and I feared she might shoot dead him on the spot.

Jimmy added some icing to a very bad cake when he nodded toward Suzi and told Angela, "It was jus' bidness. Dere was nottin' between me an' her. I used her ta fine out what dese two was upta. Dat's all."

The Chihuahua appeared placated. Suzi wasn't. She said coldly, "Gretchen is just about to come back to haunt you." She waved the gun for them to move. "Let's all take a trip downstairs to the laundry room."

"W-w-why the laundry room?" Ed asked.

"Oh, the thought of a little soap and water scare you, Eddie?" She waved the gun back and forth in front of the group when she warned them, "If you don't want to cooperate, we'll shoot you all right here. There already were bodily fluids on the kitchen floor, but I don't notice any damage to the tile. I'm guessing it will withstand a quantity of blood."

The Chihuahua whimpered loudly at the prospect, and Ed was stunned to silence. Jimmy smirked, and Suzi went after it.

"The look on your face tells me you don't care. No problem," she told him. "I'll lock them in the basement, come back upstairs, and shoot your smug ass. You already died once in this kitchen. The second time will be a charm."

Jimmy folded his arms across his chest. He still was not going to budge. At that point, I wondered if Suzi actually would take The Chihuahua and Ed to the basement, return upstairs, and execute Jimmy. It seemed so when she raised the pistol to Jimmy's face and cocked the hammer."

The Chihuahua saved the day. She scooted between the gun and Jimmy, turned and pushed him toward the basement door. "C'mon, baby," she said. "She's doesn't want to kill any of us. It's not her style, but who knows what she might do to you if you make her angry enough. Let's go downstairs."

Jimmy didn't like it, but he complied. He turned and walked toward the basement door. He was about to head downstairs when Suzi stopped him.

"Nice try, Jimmy. You'd like to be the first downstairs so you could maybe get inside the laundry room, lock the door, and make a phone call? You wouldn't care if these two got shot as long as you lived, would you?"

To all three, she commanded, "Step away from the door and wait until I instruct you to go downstairs." To The Chihuahua, she said, "Ed's still bleeding. Get another dish towel and re-wrap his hand."

Jimmy and Ed stepped to the side. After the little woman did as instructed and was back in line, Suzi said to me, "Go into the basement and wait for us. Give yourself room at the bottom of the stairs. I don't want one of these idiots falling on you when they come down. Keep your gun on them. I'll send them slowly and one at a time, and I'll bring up the rear."

I was concerned as to what was going to happen when everyone was in the laundry room. Suzi read the concern on my face and whispered, "Don't worry. From this point on, this will be a bloodless coup."

Relieved that I wasn't going to be asked to shoot anyone or witness same, I headed for the stairs. There was a switch just inside the door, and I flipped it. The light above the stairs went on.

"Let me know when you have all of the downstairs lights on. I will send them down," Suzi told me.

I went down the stairs. There was a wall switch just above the handrail. I flipped it, and overhead lights went on. "All set," I called to Suzi.

"Sending them down. Step back and keep your gun pointed at them," she called down. I heard her say to the trio. "Just like grammar school. Go in order of height. Chihuahua, Ed, and Jimmy. Move. Slowly and deliberately."

The stairway groaned is it began to accept weight. There was a slight creak as The Chihuahua appeared first. The stairs sang slightly louder as Ed descended. Before I saw Jimmy, I heard Suzi call out. "A thought just crossed my mind. If I shoot Jimmy, and he falls on the other two and crushes them, it'll take only one bullet to get rid of all three of them." The comment cause The Chihuahua and Ed to look back over their shoulders. The stairway let out a prolonged series of cries as Jimmy descended.

When all three had reached the bottom of the stairs, I said to the trio, "Suzi has quite a sense of humor, doesn't she?"

Suzi was descending the stairs and heard me. She said, "Maybe I was kidding. Maybe I wasn't. Let's find out what other kinds of fun I have in mind." After she had joined us, she looked at me and asked, "Can you keep them covered?"

"Like a warm blanket," I assured her.

"Much better than they deserve. Okay, I am going to disappear for a few minutes, and what I am about to tell you is no joke. If any or all of them try anything, you absolutely must shoot them. If you don't, and they regain control or escape, well, do I need to explain what might happen?"

She didn't. I nodded.

Suzi opened the door to what I guessed was the laundry room and stepped inside. After a few minutes, she emerged. "Okay, I've got it."

"What's the plan?" I asked.

Suzi stepped toward me and whispered loudly enough for only me to hear, "I'm going to bind and gag these bozos and lock them inside. We're going to make our escape with the money and some artworks. My colleagues at the F.B.I. will receive an anonymous call about three suspicious characters in a basement laundry room at this location. By the time everything gets sorted out, if it ever is, we'll be long gone. I'll be re-instated, and we'll have a few perks the F.B.I. need know about. Are you okay with that?"

I looked her squared in the eyes and held out my fist for her to bump. "Very okay," I assured her.

After she reciprocated, Suzi stepped to the door of the laundry room and turned the doorknob. "This door locks from the outside. Where is the key, Jimmy?"

Jimmy pursed his lips. He pondered. Suzi was ready for him this time. She raised the gun and pointed it at The Chihuahua's forehead.

The little woman shrieked. Jimmy nodded toward the wall and said, "Hangin' on a nail."

Suzi looked to the spot Jimmy had nodded, stepped toward it, and retrieved the key. She inserted it into the lock. She said, "Again, we're going to do this one at a time." To The Chuhuahua, she said, "You first. Inside."

Suzi handed me her gun. "Same scenario. Any issues. Shoot 'em."

I had a gun in each hand. Jimmy and Ed stared at me. I'm sure they were wondering how they could get the drop on me, but it was too risky. Suzi and The Chihuahua disappeared into the laundry room.

After a few minutes, Suzi re-appeared and motioned with the gun. "You're next, Ed. Inside."

Still holding the towel in front of his private part, his right hand bleeding through the towel around it, Ed slowly walked inside the laundry room. I wasn't concerned that he might try anything with Suzi. Ed was a lightweight who had to be weakened even further by the loss of blood.

After they disappeared, Jimmy whisper-growled to me, "You got bot' guns. Lock dem' inna laundry room 'n help me escape. Dere's annuda half a million bucks in that case upstairs. All yours if ya' help me escape."

My only response was a shake of the head.

Jimmy knew time was running out. He upped the offer. This time the tactic was growl-pleading. "I got more'n a half million stashed. Lots more. I can get ya more dough. C'mon, kid. I always liked ya. Whaddya say?"

"You were going to kill me and destroy my reputation after my death by leaving evidence that I was behind the stolen art operation. You fooled me once, Jimmy. You know the axiom."

Suzi emerged for the second time. She asked, "What did Jimmy offer you to help him escape? All of the money upstairs and more, I'll bet."

"He claims to have more money than Bill Gates, and says I can have half, plus he will throw in the whereabouts of Jimmy Hoffa," I told her.

"And you resisted? I'm astonished! The money is one thing, but to know what happened to Hoffa! Had he offered that to me upstairs, I might have taken it."

To Jimmy, she said, "Always play your best cards first, fatso. Now you could be bunking with Hoffa instead of revealing his whereabouts, and how about that? Another disappearance of a big time crook named Jimmy, and no one ever would know they're together for all eternity."

Jimmy was so disappointed that he wasn't going to be able to pull of one more re-incarnation or escape that he simply hung his head. For the first time in all of the years I'd known him, he appeared defeated. He lumbered inside of the laundry room. Suzi hesitated.

"It's going to take me a little longer to tie up big boy. After I do, we'll be on our way." She walked over, threw her arms around my neck, and kissed me. "You were so great in this. You know, when I first met you at B.O. High, I figured you for just an average Joe. I very much underestimated you."

She turned me loose, pivoted, and strode inside the laundry room. I followed to the doorway and watched her as she began to tie up Jimmy. When I was satisfied she was completely focused on Jimmy and not at all paying attention to yours truly, I walked over, quietly locked the laundry room door, and eased it closed. I dropped the key into my pocked and walked up the stairs.

Chapter 31
Cutting Suzi From the Caper

At first I was elated that Suzi brought her gun and had been able to turn the tables on Jimmy and company. I didn't let on, but my elation turned to skepticism as I began to understand precisely how it would turn out.

Along the way, questions raced through my mind. Atop the list: why didn't Suzi, and I'm borrowing from Ed here, pop a pill into them? She certainly had the motivation after the murder of Gretchen and their gleeful comments about it. Shooting them would have been simpler than taking them into custody. Bang. Bang. Bang. Three strikes and they'd have been out of there for eternity, and neither Suzi nor yours truly ever would be concerned they were after us. Not that I condoned murders or would have wanted any part of them. Call that a contradiction. I didn't want Suzi to shoot them, but I believed it very odd that anyone as angry Suzi professed to be would not pull the trigger.

There also was the matter of practicality. If their lives were to be spared, why would Suzi leave all three tied up? Even if she did notify the authorities, when they were taken into custody, their versions of the story would include the events that preceded their being bound and gagged. Jimmy's story might include a wild version of the stolen artwork and money in which Suzi and I actually were the masterminds behind the stolen art ring. That caused me to wonder about yet another detail.

If Suzi truly wanted to avenge her friend and F.B.I. partner Gretchen, the best thing she could have done would have been to ensure the three immediately were taken into custody and charged. She had the goods on them, and she had me as a witness to their admissions of guilt. Call me naïve and old fashioned, but I still believed F.B.I. agents were straight, not cut from the same cloth as the criminals they sought to put behind bars. Sure I told Suzi that I was down with her plan to take money and artwork. What I actually thinking was there would be no way we could get away with it.

Suzi was supposed to be off of the caper. The first thing her F.B.I. superiors would asked her would be, "What were you doing there?" It could get worse from there. A real F.B.I. agent would know that, which led to the biggest reason I locked Suzi inside the laundry room.

From the time I'd fled Jimmy's with a fortune in cash, everything had been set up to get it back from me. Jimmy and Suzi knew where I was and what I was doing all along. They knew I had stashed the money. It was a matter of how to get it back from me. There was my chance meeting The Chihuahua at a bar. Me spotting Gretchen outside of my building, but her never knowing I was on to her was ridiculous. Blowing up Suzi and Gretchen's unit was extreme. I wondered whether Jimmy, The Chihuahua, and Ed knew neither Gretchen nor Suzie were inside when the bomb detonated.

Even if Suzi and Jimmy weren't in cahoots, they could be again at some point. It was business, and business had been good for them. Why would they not return to some form of business as usual? Once they learned the whereabouts of the money I had taken, my usefulness would be over. My ending would not be anywhere as embarrassing as being found tied up naked in a basement laundry room. It might have been glamorous: in a Las Vegas hotel suite or on an exotic beach. Suzi would step away for a few minutes, never to return. I would be abandoned as I reclined on a chaise lounge poolside, the ice in the two mai tais I ordered melting as I waited for Suzi to return. Or Suzi would slip away just before sunrise while I was in the deep, peaceful sleep that follows love making. Law enforcement would burst into our expensive hotel suite and take me into custody.

Whatever the scenario, the results would be the same.

Suzi continued to bang on the laundry room door and call out to me. She spoke to me, not angrily, but reasonably, and that was calculated and smart. Temptation rose within me. I took a deep breath. Fool me once, shame on you. Fool me twice, shame on me. Fool me continuously? That might be one for The Chihuahua to explain with one of her malaprops. Had I allowed it to play out, it would have been that ridiculous. Neither Suzi nor Jimmy would need to kill me. I would have died of embarrassment and shame. Thus it came down to winning and losing, and it was not a tough call to make.

I walked up the stairs.

Standing in Jimmy's kitchen, I thought about what I would need to escape cleanly. As in my first successful escape from Jimmy's, I needed a dish towel. I removed one from the same drawer I'd seen The Chihuahua access. Afterward, I wiped my prints from its handle. I had both guns, and I didn't want to leave them. I could dump them in a sewer or a body of water later. I set them down before I walked to the living room and to the front door. The switch for the front porch light was there, and I flipped it on and off. After doing so, I watched out the window for a return signal. It came quickly from a car parked not far down the street. I was not certain, but it appeared to be a Mercedes.

I picked up the phone and dialed. "9-1-1. What's your emergency?" asked an emotionless female voice.

"I'm calling to report a dangerous situation in my neighborhood. While walking my dog, across the street I saw a tall blond woman with a gun. She was standing next to what appeared to be a silver Mercedes. Sorry, it's dark and I just wanted to get away from her. So I couldn't see the plate. Can you send someone?"

The dispatcher asked for my location, and I provided it. She asked for my name, and I declined. She said police were on the way.

I watched out the window as I spoke. All remained quiet and motionless for another thirty seconds. That was the time it took the first police cruiser to arrive from The Great Dane's six o'clock. The second arrived shortly thereafter from her twelve o'clock. The Great Dane was hemmed in. One officer exited each cruiser and cautiously approached her car. I could see each officer had an elbow cocked and a hand near the gun in his holster.

The Great Dane had an escape plan. It was daring and explosive, and it played out quickly. No sooner had the officers neared her car than she started the engine and turned on the headlights. I saw the officers flinch, but before they could react decisively, the engine revved. She had parked just ahead of a driveway and with ample space to drive onto the sidewalk, and that was exactly what she did in reverse for perhaps one hundred feet before re-entering the street via another driveway and at an increasing rate of speed. It was as spectacular to watch as it was dangerous to perform because the Mercedes, and it must have be doing eighty when its wheels hit left the sidewalk and hit the street. The car bounced slightly, zigzagged until its tires gripped the street, and zoomed off. The police officers appeared to say something into shoulder radios as they ran back to their vehicles, jumped inside, activated their emergency lights, and sped after her.

Suzi was pounding on the door a bit harder. I heard the word "please" as I watched the police lights disappear, and it hurt me. Don't beg Suzi, I thought. You're a winner. You'll figure a way out of this, but it won't involve me.

I hesitated to be certain no other police vehicles appeared before I made my own escapeBefore walking out of the front door and into the dark night, I quickly wiped clean anything I might have touched. When I exited, I took the guns, which I had wrapped inside a bath towel I'd found in a hall closet. . Unlike the first time, I wasn't interested in money. I took just one keepsake by which to remember Jimmy. As for Suzi, I had some indelible memories, one of which was her pounding and calling to me as a walked out of the front door.

Epilogue

Because I enjoyed residing in the Gold Coast, I did not return to my house to live after the repairs were complete. Instead I contacted a real estate agent and listed it. I lived at The Deco until the sale was finalized. Afterwards I used the proceeds plus some of Jimmy's money to purchase a condominium in a high rise building overlooking Lake Michigan and Lincoln Park. I looked at quite a few units before I settled on one. The clincher for me was the spectacular view.

I did not attempt to return to my job at B.O. High. Going back there would have been denying positive change or worse. It would have been reclaiming my old life and failure. I had some good memories from my time working there, but I also had some bad ones plus a late revelation: I had been set up.

Jimmy needed a patsy to take the fall for his something. Or maybe he was lining me up for when that day came. I was betting with him. He must have mentioned to someone that he needed someone naïve, a patsy. Guess who drew that lucky number? It was yours truly, the guy living *la vida loco*: running office pools and taking bets from colleagues on campus during school hours.

Now who could have set me up?

Anyway, that was why I didn't blame the administration for my firing. I walked right into the trap. Shame on me, and lessons learned. When you don't walk the straight and narrow, you'd better keep your eyes wide open. If you get a second chance, stay on the straight and narrow.

Remaining on the straight and narrow was why I used some of Jimmy's money for the down payment on my new place, I had not planned to keep one penny of it until I learned he planned to kill me and let me posthumously take the fall for one of his dirty deeds. That changed my thinking. I am proud to say that unlike Jimmy, I did some very good things with his money. Among the beneficiaries of Jimmy's generosity was Babe. I went to the police station where she was booked and obtained a copy of the police report with her address. I mailed Babe three stacks of hundreds.

I got a kick out of returning to the Holiday Inn Express at Burr Ridge, walking in, and handing three stacks to that desk clerk who was up to her eyeballs in debt. After I walked out without a word, she chased me to the parking lot, jumped on my back and began kissing my head and neck. She was so happy. When I finally convinced her to let me go, I told her, "Je suis fini." She began to cry and was so choked up that at first she couldn't utter a thank you. After a few moments, he put her hands to her lips, then to her heart and extended them toward me. "Vous etez un homme bon. Toutes les benedictions a vous," she said sincerely.

That moment was heartwarming, and I was moved. Yet it was time to move on. In English, I reminded her, "You're still not a millionaire. You'd better go back to work before you are fired."

As for Jimmy, Ed, and The Chihuahua, they remain in prison. In what may have been the fasted judicial process in Cook County history, they were convicted of faking Jimmy's death and all things pertaining to it. They were not charged with blowing up a unit in a high rise building in an attempt to murder two people. Nor were they charged for smuggling, brokering or possession of so much as the one piece of stolen art that was found inside Jimmy's home.

Jimmy's crime was an offense not on the books: stupidity. In Cook County, that is defined as being caught in a situation so egregiously incriminating that it can't be fixed.

The people who helped Jimmy pretend to be dead – judges, clerks, law enforcement officials – were very upset. No way were they going down for helping Jimmy, and they did not appreciate the spotlight shining on them. Cockroaches prefer the dark. They made sure Jimmy was punished for breaking the First Commandment of Cook County: *Thou Shalt Not Get Caught.* Understanding that he had to take his lumps, Jimmy took full responsibility. He implicated no one. He apologized to everyone and admitted that he'd taken advantage of the system and those who worked so honestly and diligently to uphold it. Because he did, and undoubtedly because he used a portion of the fortune he had stashed the required officials, Cook County law enforcement and its judiciary made sure Jimmy was charged and convicted of only with the lesser crimes.

Jimmy claimed he had no idea how a copy of Vermeer's *The Girl With the Pearl Earring* found its way into his home, and the authorities covered him by sweeping his crime under the rug. There was a funny exchange during the press conference that followed Jimmy's arrest. A reporter said, "If that's a copy, it's a fabulous copy. Is there any chance it's the real thing and the one at The Hague is an imposter?" The law enforcement spokesperson explained, "That painting is a copy. There's no question. We had it analyzed. We checked with Interpol. There is no report that a copy was stolen. We can't charge someone for having a copy of a famous work of art. What crime could we charge him with, having good taste but not being able to afford the original? For all we know, the guy's an amateur artist, and he painted it himself."

Jimmy was good, but he was not that good. Still, the media bought it. No one brought it up *The Girl With the Pearl Earring* again for a while.

The truth about Jimmy would have come out had Ed or The Chihuahua turned on him, but they didn't. The Chihuahua offered a tearful apology and expressed regret "for helping the man she loves seek a new life through death." It was classic Chihuahua. Apparently she couldn't come up with an appropriate malaprop and went for confusion. Ed silently reaffirmed his loyalty when he pleaded guilty and refused to testify or answer questions. I suspect Ed enjoys prison life for its simplicity and that he may regret being paroled. It wouldn't surprise me if he shanked someone just to get more time.

Because Jimmy wasn't nailed for smuggling and brokering stolen art, Larry, the assistant football coach from B.O. High whose fulltime job was airport luggage handler, was not charged. Suzi had confided that Larry helped Jimmy move product in and out. There was some price to pay, however. Larry disappeared. There was no word as to whether he went into hiding or was the victim of foul play. The attorney who created Jimmy's pre-mortem trust got a slap on the wrist. He lost his law license for one year, but he received no jail time.

That was it for Jimmy and everyone connected to him.

As for those on the fringe, The Great Dane's legal situation was similar to Jimmy's. When you're dumb enough to be implicated for a rap that can't be fixed, you will be a fall guy, although in this case it was a fall girl. Someone had be charged when a unit in a high rise unit blows up, and one of the occupants uses the act to fake their death. That was the crime for which the Great Dane was indicted. The authorities could not make it stick, however, because they'd already announced the explosion was due to a gas leak, not a murder plot, and unlike Jimmy, she had not taken steps to legally have herself declared dead. Thus The Great Dane beat that rap.

She was convicted of carrying a concealed weapon without a F.O.I.D card, for eluding, for beating up two of the police officers who finally cornered her after she fled Jimmy's, and for some small potatoes things that municipalities don't like, such as driving on their sidewalks. Sentenced to six years in state prison, The Great Dane took over the toughest female gang at the facility. Her time has been extended for its various illegal activities such as beating up guards and being in possession of contraband.

Not what I would have expected the outcome to be for an FBI agent, but then again, I'm only a history teacher.

Regarding FBI agent Chen, I can't say that Suzi misses her partner because I do not know what happened to Suzi.

The arrests of and legal proceedings pertaining to Jimmy, Ed, The Chihuahua, and The Great Dane appeared in news reports. There never was mention of a Suzi Chen or anyone else being suspected, arrested, charged, or sought for questioning regarding anything that happened. There were no reports of the FBI or any of its agents being involved.

What I suspect transpired was that Suzi freed herself from the laundry room and went upstairs to assess the situation. I was gone, and so was The Great Dane. In a precise and very timely manner, Suzi arranged to take all of the stolen art Jimmy had in the house except one piece. I left the secret panel open so that she would find it.

If she was able to broker Vermeer's *The Concert*, *Portrait of a Young Man by Raphael*, and *The Storm on the Sea of Galilee* by Rembrandt, well, should she have received so much as a fraction of what they are worth – plus the money she took from Jimmy's – Suzi is living in safe and luxurious seclusion in a castle in Europe, in a mountain chalet in Switzerland, or in a mansion in Beverly Hills.

Although she did not arrest them or take them into custody herself, I am certain FBI agent Chen was responsible for Jimmy, Ed, and The Chihuahua being discovered and arrested and for leaving me a very important message.

According to news reports, the police and the media received an anonymous tip that the bar owner who reportedly had been killed in his own kitchen actually was alive in the laundry room of his home and there was stolen art there. The trio had been tied up there two days before authorities and arrived and took them custody. News crews filmed them doing so. Seeing the three of them perp walked out of Jimmy's wrapped in towels followed by cops carrying the fake Vermeer and the nude of The Chihuahua was a hoot.

I'm sure that tip came from Suzi, who is too smart to be caught doing anything and always seemed one step ahead of everybody. Heck, I still marvel that I was able to lock her inside Jimmy's laundry room, and I hope that if we meet again, we'll be able to laugh about it. Not that Suzi will come looking for me. Not unless she decides she also wants the money I took from Jimmy, but why should she? It would be chicken feed to Suzi. The Vermeer she took was valued at $200 million.

Speaking of Vermneers, the painting left behind must have been a very good copy is what I thought at first. If it didn't have the value of the others, why should Suzi take it? It was a well-known fact that the real *Girl With the Pearl Earring* was in the Mauritshuis museum. On the other hand, Suzi was smart. Everything she did was for a reason. That copy was so good that it might have fetched a hefty price. So why not take it? She could have left something else or nothing. Why did she leave the fake Vermeer?

I thought about it, and after I thought about it long enough, I came up with the answer. The Vermeer wasn't a great copy, and the message was that I needed to use it save both of our lives. If I did, we would live happily ever after.

I visited Jimmy in prison. I needed to have a conversation with the man who was going to have me killed and who still might.

A much leaner version of Jimmy entered a small room sat down in the chair at a countertop separated from me in my room by thick glass. Jimmy had a shaved head, and he appeared to have lost, well, I couldn't even guess how much weight he'd lost. He wasn't slim, but he no longer was Buddha. His face was skinny jowly, and the prison garb hung on him. Jimmy appeared older, yet he looked better, more healthy. I was happy for him until he sarcastically growled into the phone, "Tanks fer comin' ta see me, kid. Appreciate it." He folded his arms across his chest, smirked, and waited.

Jimmy's greeting told me everything I needed to know. He was going to have me killed. Not until he or whomever he hired retrieved the money, but eventually. Jimmy had covered himself by announcing he was glad to see me. If the phones we were using were tapped, as I was counting on, it would be on record that Jimmy and I were friends, and that he had no reason to kill me. That would have been his claim if and when my body was discovered. I wasn't going to give him a chance at either.

"I'm here to come clean, Jimmy. I just want to say again that I never took any money from you. Anything that disappeared from your home, well, it wasn't me. I hope you'll believe me, and we can be on good terms. If so, I'll come back to visit. Do you need anything?"

Jimmy's smirk turned into a pucker. His body tensed, and he inhaled. He emitted a low growl. He scratched his scalp. He spoke in code. "Uh huh. Do I need anyting? Dat's a hot one." He grimaced and added, "Nobody said nuthin' 'bout no money. You got any ideas 'bout anybody took anyting elsa mine?"

He was referring to the stolen art, and he wanted me to speak in code. Well, we were going to talk about the art and the money, but there wasn't going to any code. I acted innocent. I shrugged. "No idea of who would take any of your art work, Jimmy. As for the money, I heard some rumors. I wouldn't want to name any names. To implicate someone based on a rumor would be wrong."

I added, "I did hear there were some sizable charitable donations made in your name." This was true. After I'd made the deposit on my new place, I made anonymous cash donations to local charities. Jimmy finally had done something good with his money.

Jimmy wasn't feeling generous. He didn't like hearing that his money was gone forever, and he wanted the name of the perpetrator. He took a deeper breath. His growl was more angry. I stoked the fire.

"I was sorry to learn the IRS is going to take everything from you, Jimmy. The bar and your house. That fake Vermeer and the nude of Angela."

Jimmy began to turn red. "Waddaya talkin 'bout? Da IRS? Who sed dat? Where'd you get dat? Who's talkin 'bout me? You talkin' ta anybody ''bout me?"

"Not me," I assured him before I stuck the needle in deeper. "Any idea what you might do when you get out. Maybe go back to work on the beer truck? You won't have any money. You won't be able to go back into the bar business."

If Jimmy was anything, he was arrogant and egomaniacal. Prison couldn't change that, and I'd played on it.

"If ya tol' me who walked outta my house with 'bout half million dollars, den I would have some money, wouldn' I?" he told me in a hiss growl.

I shook my head. "Can't do it, Jimmy. I'm worried what happened to your previous fall guys and was going to happen to me will happen to them." I interjected, "Is Ed the grim reaper? He took care of them, and he was going to take care of me? Although I don't know why I should worry about Ed. He's in jail."

Jimmy's growl was menacing. His graying eyebrows narrowed. "He ain't gonna be in jail forever. Neider'm I. You ever tink 'bout dat?"

"Why should I? You're broke. When you are paroled, Ed will abandon you because you can't afford to carry him anymore. Ed was only with you for the money. You guys are done. There is nothing to worry about." I shrugged my shoulders to emphasize that I wasn't worried.

Jimmy exploded. He pounded the counter with his free hand. "Dat what you tink! Dat I don't have millions more stashed! Dat when I get out the same thing happened to doze udder stooges won' happen ta you! Lissen ta you! Ain't you fulla yerself!"

He banged on the counter again, and it jumped. "Angela was right. You're soft. When she suggested you, she tol' me you'd be da poifec' patsy. What's gonna happena you'll happen so fast ya won' know what hit ya!" Again he slammed on the counter. "Bam! Jus like dat! Dead! For da whole world ta see!"

The door behind him opened and two guards walked into the room, but Jimmy was oblivious to them. He continued to rale.

"No money? Fake Va'meer. Ha! I got millions stashed, and dat painting is the real McCoy. D'ere holdin' it for me! Da one in dat museum whereva, da Neverlands! Dat's da fake! I got da real one, 'n I'll make millions off it!"

I wanted to thank Jimmy for the malapropism and that his beloved Angela would be proud, but there was not time. The guards came up behind Jimmy, grabbed him under the arms, and pulled him out of the chair and backwards out of the door. Going in reverse did not stop Jimmy from screaming.

"You tell dat Chen broad I wan' my artwork an' my money back. When I get outta here, I'm gonna use every penny I got stashed to find youz 'n killa ya bot'! You got dat! You got dat! You're gonna see me again, you no-good l'il punk!"

The door closed. There was no more screaming. Jimmy was gone

The authorities must have been listening to our conversation because not long afterward it was announced that Jimmy was indicted for murder, art smuggling, and money laundering. Ed and The Chihuahua were indicted as co-conspirators. All three await trial. I was called in for questioning, but all I could tell them was I had been hired by Jimmy to perform a task I never started, that I had seen large sums of money at Jimmy's, and that I had seen works of art. I added that I didn't know if the art was real or what happened to it or the money. Technically that was true. I no longer knew who had the money, and I didn't know for sure if Suzi Chen had taken the art. Or if her real name was Suzi Chen. Or if she was an FBI agent.

All I knew was that she was the perfect woman for me and always would be whoever she was.

My new life has worked out better than I imagined. I was able to find another teaching position, and I work at a high school not far from my home. I am still in love, and it was love at first sight. Now that I understand it better, I do not plan ever again to be apart from her. Thus it is my hope that we can remain together for as long as I live. I do not know if I could go on without laying my hands softly upon her, without holding her in my arms and gently cradling her, without gazing upon her beauty.

Fortunately, my love and I now have a great relationship. At least once a day, I press a button under an end table in my bedroom. A secret panel slides open – a la the one Jimmy had in his home - and I remove the box which contains the object of my affection. I remove the most beautiful thing I have ever seen, place her on a table, and stare at her. Then I pick her up, hold her, and walk around with her cradled in my arms.

In my wildest dreams, I never imagined I ever would be in possession of not a merely Faberge Egg, but one of the most valuable and sought after Faberge Eggs in history, one that has been missing for over one hundred years, the *Alexander III Commemorative Egg*. While I do not know how he managed to acquired it, I do marvel that he did so, and I greatly appreciate it.

Thank you, Jimmy.

About the Author

Joseph Thomas Gatrell is a writer, teacher, exercise fanatic, and information addict. A former altar boy, he is a survivor of 12 years of Catholic school education. He notes, however, that the only time a member of the clergy laid a hand on him was when a nun sucker punched him when he was in the 5th grade. Joseph is a graduate of Mount Carmel High School of Chicago and Valley City State College, and apparently he enjoyed college so much that it took him six years to graduate. Joseph lives in the Gold Coast of Chicago with his roomate, Speedy the Beagle.